THE CAMP-FIRE
SLEEPOVER

The Sleepover Gang

Louise   Jo   Charlie   Alex

Charlie is building up the suspense before she tells
her story . . .

Louise is nervous about staying out all night . . .

Alex is longing to hear about the headless
horseman . . .

Jo is obsessed with a boy called Stephen,
but it won't stop her listening to Charlie's story . . .

The Camp-fire Sleepover

Sharon Siamon

Hodder
Children's
Books

a division of Hodder Headline plc

To Abbi Slater

Acknowledgements: The story that Charlie tells in this book is based on the many legends of a headless horseman told in the mountains of New England. Among these, Washington Irving's *The Legend of Sleepy Hollow* is probably the best known.

First published in Great Britain in 1997
by Hodder Children's Books

The right of Sharon Siamon to be identified as the Author of this Work has been asserted by her in accordance with the Copyright, Designs and Patents Act 1988.

10 9 8 7 6 5 4 3 2 1

A CIP catalogue record for this title is available from the British Library

ISBN 0 340 67279 X

Typeset by Palimpsest Book Production Limited, Polmont, Stirlingshire

Printed and bound in Great Britain by Clays Ltd, St Ives plc

Hodder Children's Books
a division of Hodder Headline plc
338 Euston Road
London NW1 3BH

One

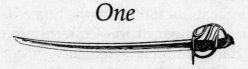

'He laughed at me!' Jo moaned. Her slender shape paced back and forth in front of the dancing flames of the camp-fire. 'I fell off the horse, right in front of Stephen, and he just stood there, laughing!'

She stopped pacing to glare at Alex, Charlie and Louise. 'You three don't even care!' The other members of the sleepover gang were stretched on the sand around the blazing fire. The four of them had been out pony trekking all day at a nearby riding stable. Now they were back at Charlie's comfortable old cottage, on the lakeshore.

'Falling off a horse is nothing to be ashamed of,' Charlie shrugged, 'and don't listen to Stephen Piggott. He's such a goof! Come on, Jo, sit down.'

Jo plunked down on the sand. 'I've never been so embarrassed in my life,' she groaned. 'I ride like a pro all day, and then, when we get back to the stables, the horse jerks to one side, and I fly off and land at Stephen's feet like a sack of cement!'

'Forget about falling off the horse.' Charlie shook her finger at Jo. 'Concentrate on the important thing. *Do we have enough food to last all night?* I brought marshmallows, drinks, a whole bag of chocolate fudge finger cookies . . .' For Charlie, food was always the important thing.

'Who cares about food?' Louise sighed happily. 'It's just great to be together.' She smiled around at the three familiar faces – Jo with her bright blue eyes and long brown hair, Charlie with her mischievous face, Alex with her wide grin and mop of curls. This was the best part of the summer, Louise thought. They still had two whole weeks before school started. She threw herself back on her sleeping bag and stared up at the darkening sky, where pinpricks of stars were just starting to appear.

Alex reached for a stick of firewood. 'Louise is right,' she agreed. 'I've always wanted to have a camp-fire sleepover – to sleep out under the stars on a warm night like this.' She added her stick to the fire

2

and a stream of sparks shot into the air.

Charlie bounced up and danced around the camp-fire. 'Who said anything about *sleeping*?' she cried. 'It's my turn to tell a ghost story. After you hear this one, you might not sleep all night!'

Louise gave a shudder and burrowed deeper in her bag. Suddenly, the night didn't seem so warm. What would it be like, out here in the dark, with only the fire, and no walls to keep them safe? 'You're always saying you don't believe in ghosts,' she shivered.

'Normally I don't,' Charlie agreed. 'But up here it's easy to believe in the unbelievable.' She gestured at the shadowy hills around the lake. 'There are lots of old stories. Do you know there is supposed to be a lake monster right here in this lake?'

There was silence for a moment, broken only by the crackling of the flames. Then Charlie tossed a stone toward the dark water and they heard a hollow *plop* as it sank.

'Well,' said Jo, at last. 'Tell us about this lake monster.'

Charlie came back to crouch by the fire again. 'People say it's like a huge snake, with eyes on stalks,' she began. 'But it can only see in the dark.'

'Why?' Alex asked. She put another stick on the fire.

'Because the lake is so deep that the sun never reaches the underwater caves where it lives.' Charlie went on. 'The lake monsters have lived down there for thousands of years. They only come up to the surface at night . . . to feed!'

Louise gave a shudder. 'Wha . . . what do they eat?'

'Anything they can catch,' Charlie whispered. 'They just slither up far enough to see what's on the shore. Then they snatch it in their huge jaws, and . . . *crunch*!'

'Stop!' Louise cried. 'I get the picture. Maybe we should sleep a bit further from the edge of the water.' She scrunched her sleeping bag further up the sandy shore. 'You're not going to tell us one of those old lake monster stories tonight, are you?'

Charlie stared across the fire at Louise's pale face. 'No. My story is about a horse and ghostly rider.'

'Not horses!' Jo groaned. 'I never want to see, or hear, or *think* about a horse again as long as I live.'

4

'Just because you fell off?' Charlie peered into Jo's face. 'You didn't even hurt yourself. The horse was standing still!'

'That does it! I'm not going to stay here and be made fun of.' Jo stood up and stalked away, down towards the water and the dock.

'You shouldn't tease Jo,' Louise protested. 'Her pride was hurt. She feels bad because Stephen laughed at her. I think she kind of likes him.'

'This isn't like her,' Alex added. 'Jo is usually in the middle of things, getting us all organised – she's crazy about ghost stories.'

'You're right,' Charlie nodded. 'Jo, come on,' she shouted. 'There's tons of junk food here, and I'm going to tell a truly terrifying story. I promise you'll love it.'

'In a minute . . .' Jo called back. In the gathering darkness they could just make out her slim figure, poised on the edge of the floating dock. 'Is that Stephen's cottage down there? Where I see lights?' They saw her point out over the water.

Charlie suddenly leaped to her feet. 'Jo! Step back! Watch out! . . . *Oh no!*'

The dock suddenly tipped violently, as if a huge hand had seized it. There was an enormous *splash*! as Jo hit the water on the far side.

'The lake monster!' Louise cried.

The sleepover gang were on their feet, running towards the dock.

'Jo, are you all right?'

'Has it got you by the leg?'

'Let us help you . . .'

As they crowded on to the floating dock the other three could see Jo's wet head and white face break the surface of the water. 'I'm fine,' she choked, spitting out a huge mouthful of water.

'Swim round to the ladder at the end,' Charlie shouted directions. 'Don't try to climb out on the side or you'll flip us all in. My parents keep saying they're going to fix this dock so it won't tip but they never do. It's fine as long as you don't stand near the edge.'

'Come on, Jo,' Alex kneeled down and reached out a hand. 'I've got you.' She pulled Jo, sopping wet in her clothes, on to the dock.

'I feel like such an idiot,' Jo muttered, wringing out her dripping T-shirt. 'That's twice in one day I've made a fool of myself.'

Just then a hideous laugh floated up over the lake, freezing them all to the spot.

'What's that?' Jo cried, grabbing Louise by the arm. The four of them stared out over the darkening lake.

Two

'Listen!' Charlie said.

The laugh came again, closer this time. It sounded like a cross between a cry of pain and a witch's cackle, floating eerily out of the darkness.

'Is it the monster?' Louise shuddered.

'No,' Charlie laughed, 'just a bird.'

'I don't know any bird that sounds like that!' Jo was shivering in her wet clothes.

'It's a water bird – a loon,' Charlie said. 'Haven't you heard the expression, 'Laugh like a loon'? That's their *good night, sweet dreams* laugh, just before dark.'

'More like, *good night, sweet nightmares*,' Alex said. 'What a perfect intro to a ghost story. Come on, Jo. Let's get you dried off, so Charlie can start.'

Jo was shivering in her wet clothes. 'Even the loons are laughing at me,' she muttered, as they made their way back to the camp-fire.

While Jo ran up the flagstone path to Charlie's cottage to change, Louise spread the sleeping bags close to the fire. Charlie checked her cooler of drinks and supply of food, and Alex carried up a pail of water from the lake to douse any stray embers.

'Everybody got their flashlight?' Jo asked, as she came back down the path in dry clothes, into the circle of firelight. 'It's getting pitch-dark.' She warmed her cold hands at the fire. 'Charlie, your mum wants to know if we need anything.'

Charlie groaned. 'I hope you told her we were fine. I made her promise not to run down here every ten minutes to see how we're doing.'

Jo sat down beside Louise and hugged her sleeping bag round her. 'All right, Charlie, let's hear your old horse story.'

'The story I'm going to tell isn't that old,' Charlie said. 'It happened just a few years ago, and Amy Rice swears it's all true.'

'Who's Amy Rice?' Alex asked quickly.

'I met her at riding camp, up in West Chadwick, last year,' Charlie said. 'She's been coming to the camp ever since it started. Amy is a *really* good rider – even though she's so short. She looks fantastic on a horse!'

The others grinned at each other. Height was a sore spot with Charlie. She longed to be tall, like Alex.

'We all looked up to Amy,' Charlie went on, 'she was beautiful, with pale blonde hair like Louise's and amazing green eyes. But there was something strange about her. It was as if she was always watching for things other people couldn't see, or listening for things they couldn't hear. And one night, when we were sitting around a camp-fire just like this, she told us why.'

She looked around at them. 'I'm warning you. This story will make your hair stand on end. You may not be able to sleep.'

Louise gripped her flashlight and leaned closer to the firelight. She wouldn't think about what might be out there in the dark trees, the dark water.

Charlie sat cross-legged, her back as straight as though she were still on a horse. She tilted her head to one side as she spoke and suddenly it wasn't the joking, teasing Charlie of every day the others heard, but a different voice that drew pictures in the air.

It started when Amy Rice and her mother were driving to the Sunset Trails Riding Camp for the first time. Once they got there, Amy knew all her troubles would be over. She would have a whole summer of riding up here in these beautiful mountains.

In the meantime, she was trying not to lose her temper and get into a fight with her mother.

'I just don't want to hear that you're sick of riding and want to come home in a week,' her mother was saying, as she steered the car round the twists and turns of the mountain road. 'We've spent a fortune on this riding business. Regulation helmet, special pants and boots. Not to mention that saddle!'

Amy glanced at her pride and joy in the back seat, her new riding saddle. 'I won't get sick of it,' she said in a low voice. 'Riding is . . . different.'

'How is it different? You're always falling in love with something new. Remember skating lessons? Remember the violin?' It was starting to rain and Amy's mother switched on the wipers. 'How long will this passion for riding last?' she asked.

'For ever!' Amy cried. From the first time she'd been close enough to a horse to stroke its nose and feed it a carrot, she'd known she was born to learn to ride and perhaps even become a champion rider.

'And now there's this riding camp,' her mum went on. '*If* we ever get there . . . for heaven's sake watch for signs to West Chadwick. I hope it isn't much further. It's going to be dark soon.' The rain was coming down harder and she increased the wiper speed.

Amy sighed. One of the best things about riding camp would be a whole summer on her own. Ever since a car accident two years ago, Mum had been treating her like some kind of fragile doll. *She's afraid I'll fall off a horse and break a leg*! Amy thought. *That's the real reason she doesn't want me to ride.*

The rain was coming down in buckets by the time they reached North Chadwick. It was hard to see the small white church, the houses and street signs through the streaming windshield.

'Turn here,' Amy pointed to a road forking left. 'This must be the road to West Chadwick.'

'Are you sure?' Her mother spun the wheel and made the turn. 'I didn't see a sign.'

'It has to be,' Amy said. 'There aren't any other roads.'

The road snaked up round steep curves to the edge of town. There, the asphalt ended, and they found themselves on a narrow dirt road. It seemed to wind and twist on endlessly.

Amy peered anxiously through the pouring rain at the forest on both sides, wiping her hand over her steamy window, trying to see more clearly. She hadn't seen a house or barn for a long time. Maybe they *were* on the wrong road.

Huge maple trees met overhead. Their lower branches swung in the wind, scraping the sides of the car. The wiper blades flicked back and forth in a hopeless attempt to clear the wall of water in front of them.

Amy's mother gripped the steering wheel. 'Look at this!' she shouted over the pounding of the rain on the car roof. 'I can't see a thing. We're never going to find this ridiculous riding camp!'

'Take it easy, Mum.'

She knew her mother was nervous about

driving in bad weather. She had been driving in the rain when they had the accident. If only Dad were here to drive her to camp! As usual, he was in Southeast Asia on one of his business trips.

Now the wind thrashed furiously at the little car. Thunder boomed around them, and sheets of lightning lit up the forest. Her mother fought the wheel to hold the car on the muddy road.

Suddenly, in a brilliant flash of lightning, Amy saw something loom in the headlights. It was difficult to make out the details, but through the streaming window she could just make out the shape of a towering hooded figure on a huge black horse. It was galloping straight towards them.

'Mum, look out!' she screamed.

Charlie paused and reached for a can of fizzy orange. 'Thirsty work,' she grinned at the others as she popped the lid and took a long swig.

'Oh, don't stop now,' Jo groaned. 'You've just got started.'

'You know our Charlie,' Alex chuckled. 'When have you ever seen her go for more than ten minutes without putting something in her mouth?'

Charlie took another long pull at the drink can and gave a contented burp. 'That's better,' she said. 'Now where was I?'

Three

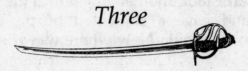

'Something was galloping towards them,' Louise shivered. 'Did they hit it?'

'It must have been a horse,' Jo muttered. 'I'm telling you, they're dangerous and unpredictable animals. One minute they're standing quietly, and the next, you're flying off their backs.'

'You have a warped view of horses,' Charlie said. 'Hand me a chocolate bar, Jo. I have to keep up my strength for this story.'

'Maybe Amy just *imagined* she saw a horse and rider,' Louise said. 'She was thinking so much about riding.'

'Why don't you let Charlie go on,' Alex suggested, putting another log on the fire. The night had closed in around them. They sat close to the camp-fire as Charlie took up the story.

* * *

Charlie wiggled back into her cross-legged position. She stared into the fire as she began to speak.

Amy saw the dark shape thunder towards them. She heard her mother scream, felt the wrench of the car as her mother swerved to avoid hitting it, and then they were sliding, spinning helplessly in the dark.

Things seemed to happen in slow motion. The horse and rider flashed before them. Amy waited for the sickening thud as they collided, but the car spun away.

They were sliding, out of control, straight for a huge tree-trunk! Amy threw her hands up in front of her face, but the car was still spinning. It grazed the tree-trunk, tipped forward violently and came to a stop.

Amy could hear the rain thudding on the car roof, the far off boom of thunder. Her heart was hammering in her chest. She had no sense of where they were, or which direction the car was pointing.

'Are you all right?' she heard her mother say.

'Yes, I think so.' She tried moving her body. This time there was no pain seeping through the stillness of shock. Just her heart thudding in her ears. 'We almost hit that horse,' she whispered.

'Or *it* nearly hit us . . .' her mother said shakily. 'Get out and take a look. We seem to be on a slant.'

Amy undid her seat belt, opened the door on her side, and scrambled out. The rain hit her like an ice-cold shower. She slid down a thick bank of loose gravel to where the car's front end was buried. What she saw made her gasp and reach for the car for support. The gravel had saved their lives. Where it ended, the earth fell away into empty space.

They were perched on the very edge of a deep pit of some kind. Amy peered over the edge and shivered violently. She could not see the bottom. A little further and they would be down there, in that huge dark hole!

'I'll try to back up,' Amy's mum called from the car window. She gunned the engine, but the wheels spun in the loose gravel. It slipped a little closer to the edge of the pit.

'STOP!' Amy screamed. 'Mum, get out of the car!'

'What on earth is the matter?' Amy's mother edged out from behind the wheel, holding her large carry-all bag over her head as protection from the driving rain. When she saw the great yawning pit in front of them she clutched Amy's arm. 'Oh, my God! Get up on the road, quick!'

They scrambled up the gravel bank, and stood shaking in the middle of the road. The wind howled through the branches of the big trees on either side and thunder boomed all around them. Amy's mother fumbled in her bag for her cell phone. 'I'll have to call a tow truck . . .'

Amy waited, her teeth chattering, while her mother punched buttons on the phone. The rain was soaking through her thin jacket and jeans.

'It seems to be completely dead!' Her mother shook the phone. 'We must be out of the calling zone . . .' She switched it off and gazed at Amy in despair.

'Maybe the rider we almost hit will come back and help us,' Amy shouted. She peered down the road where the horse had disappeared. A sudden fork of lightning struck so close it shook the ground, and a crash of thunder drowned out her words.

'Whoever it was must be out of his mind to be riding in this!' Amy's mother cried.

'Come on. There must be houses along this road.'

She handed Amy a pocket flashlight from her bag. 'Here – look for a house, a barn, anything! Maybe that horse came from the riding camp. It can't be too far.'

They began to plod through the pouring rain. The road was now just two muddy ruts. Amy shone the light over its surface, looking for something that should have been there. If a horse had ridden along this road, there should be hoof prints, deep in the mud. But there were none. She shone the light from side to side to be sure. If a horse had been galloping towards them, it had left no mark.

They struggled up a steep hill with the rain lashing their faces. Then across a bridge, and up again. Amy had never felt so wet in her life. Her shoes squelched with every step. Her jeans were plastered to her legs, making it hard to walk.

At the top of the next hill another road joined their track. Amy searched the mud for hoof prints again. There were none.

'Which way?' her mother's streaming face turned to hers.

Amy shone the light through the wall of

falling water and darkness. Nailed to the trunk of a large maple near the corner was a wooden sign. She plunged off the road, through the long wet grass to read the white letters.

SUNSET TRAILS RIDING CAMP

Four

The door of a large, run-down farmhouse opened to their frantic knocking. A very tall young man stood in the doorway. His face was tanned and his brown hair was streaked with bronze. He was dressed in a red sweater and brown riding pants.

Amy took all this in as they stood staring at each other. Then the young man's face flushed with concern. 'You're soaked. Come in!'

He offered a hand to help her mother inside. 'I'm Nicholas. Welcome to Sunset Trails!'

Nicholas looked like a man in a magazine ad, Amy thought. She stepped into the small untidy living-room. Nicholas closed the door, his golden head brushing the low door frame.

Amy's mother introduced herself. 'I'm Louise Rice, and this is my daughter, Amy. Our car is in the ditch, down the road.'

'Mother,' the bronzed young man boomed over his shoulder. 'It's Mrs Rice. They've had an accident.'

The woman who strode forward also wore riding clothes. Her dark blonde hair was flecked with grey. She thrust out her hand. 'I'm Sheila Campbell, the owner of Sunset Trails. We must get you dry. Nicholas, build up the fire . . .'

Amy saw a large stone fireplace in the back wall. Above it hung an antique sword, its blade gleaming in the firelight. Ashes and soot from the grate spilled out on to the plank floor.

'Excuse the mess,' Nicholas said. 'We've been working on the place since we moved up from Boston, but there's still lots to do . . .' He gave her a warm smile.

Amy felt her face flush red. He was so good-looking! She stumbled after her mother and Sheila Campbell to the bedrooms at the back of the house. 'I hope you find something that fits,' Sheila Campbell told Amy, opening the door of the closet. 'You look quite small.'

Amy was used to the way no one took her seriously because of her size, but it still annoyed her. 'I'm stronger than I look,' she bristled.

Sheila Campbell gave a brisk nod. 'I'm sure you are.' She picked up a sweater and pair of jeans. 'I'd better take some dry clothes to your mother.'

Amy could see the look of shock on her mother's face when they met back in the living room. Mum was a fussy housekeeper. The Sunset Trails farmhouse was anything but well-kept. A metal basin in the middle of the floor caught the drips from a leaky ceiling.

Sheila Campbell led the way to the fireplace, where a hot fire was blazing and two battered armchairs were waiting.

'How far did you walk?' Nicholas asked Amy, as she sank into one of the chairs.

'There's a very steep bank where we went off the road,' Amy told him. 'It looked like some kind of enormous pit.' She shuddered with a sudden image of their car rolling over and over into empty space.

Nicholas looked alarmed. 'It sounds as though you went off the road near the old marble quarry. How did you manage to get there?'

Amy's mother glanced at her. 'I think we took a wrong turn in North Chadwick,' she said.

'That explains it,' Nicholas shook his head. 'You must have been on the old quarry road. It hasn't been used for years.'

'And then something ran in front of us,' Amy went on. 'I think it was a horse. Mum hit the brakes and the car skidded . . .'

'Oh, no. It couldn't have been a horse,' Sheila Campbell interrupted. 'Ours are the only horses round here, and they're all stabled safely in the barn.'

'You must have seen a moose,' Nicholas added. 'There are lots of them around this year.'

Amy thought of the muddy road with no hoof prints leading back to the stable. Whatever it was had come out of nowhere!

At that moment, a gust of wind rattled the glass in the windows. Nicholas sprang to his feet. 'Speaking of horses, I'd better check that they're all right.' He put on a long raincoat and disappeared into the storm.

Amy longed to go with him. She was dying to see the barn and the Sunset Trails horses.

'I'd like to call a tow truck, if I could use your phone,' her mother was saying.

'No one will come out from town tonight,' said Sheila Campbell, shaking her head.

'You're welcome to stay. I have a spare bed, and Amy can get settled in her bunkhouse once the storm lets up.'

Amy didn't look at her mother's face. No matter how tired she was, Mum wouldn't be happy about sleeping at Sunset Trails!

Later, in the bunkhouse, Amy's mother paced the floor. 'This bunkhouse is in terrible shape. The roof is sagging and that screen door has a big hole!'

Amy thought the bunkhouse looked perfect. The shutters were closed to keep out the rain, and two small beds were spread with warm quilts.

'I'll be fine,' Amy said. 'Tomorrow there'll be another camper in here with me, and Nicholas will get the door fixed. You heard what Mrs Campbell said. Sunset Trails was abandoned for years when they bought it. It needs a lot of work.'

'I'm still not sure I can leave you here,' Amy's mother muttered.

'I know, Mum, but let's wait and see the rest of the place,' Amy begged. 'I'm sure it's lovely in the daylight.'

'Yes. We'll look around in the morning, but I'm not promising you can stay.' Her mother flipped up the hood of her borrowed raincoat, gave her a quick kiss, and left her on her own.

Amy woke up with a start, sometime in the middle of the night. The down comforter had slid off, leaving her shaking with cold. Someone was crying – it sounded like a baby.

Amy got out of bed, wrapped the down quilt round her and tiptoed across the cold floor to the window. The crying seemed to fill the night, making Amy feel lost and sad. Wouldn't someone come and help that baby? She struggled with the heavy shutter. As it swung back, and she leaned out of the open window, Amy realised the sound was just one tree branch rubbing against another, somewhere nearby.

The storm was over and a faint smoky odour hung in the still night air. Amy had no idea of the time, but she wondered if she dared to pay a visit to the barn. Why not? The rain had stopped and she was longing to see the horses! She ran back across the bare boards to her bunk, and fumbled under it for her socks and shoes.

The moon lit the way from the bunkhouse

to the big barn doors. Amy hurried through the wet grass, wondering if Nicholas might still be doing late night chores.

Nicholas, his mother had told them, was a top level competitive rider. They had bought Sunset Trails to have a place where he could train. She would learn so much, just watching him ride.

She pulled one tall wooden door open and slipped inside. Instantly, the warm sweet barn smells enveloped her. A small bare light bulb, hanging from the ceiling, gave enough light to see. Here, everything was neat and in its place. The leather tack gleamed on its hooks. Grooming tools were set out in the order they would be used – brushes, curry combs, hoof picks.

Amy stood still for a moment, until she was sure there was no one else in the barn. No one but the horses. From two rows of box stalls, on either side of a clean central corridor, came the sounds of contented animals.

Amy tiptoed to one stall and peered over the top. In the shadows, a dark bay mare with a white blaze on her forehead was standing quietly. She bobbed her head up and down, then came over to say hello.

Amy felt her heart swell as she stroked

the mare's soft nose. The little horse was so friendly and responsive. Her bright brown eyes gazed curiously at Amy, and then she bobbed her head again as if to say 'Don't stop patting me. I liked that.'

'I wish I had a treat for you,' Amy whispered. 'Next time I come I'll bring a carrot.'

She rubbed her finger over the brass name plate on the stall. 'Classy,' she breathed. 'That's a good name for you.'

At her voice there was a stamping and snorting from the next stall. A long black face peered out as if to say, 'Look at me. I'm the important horse around here.'

Amy went to the next stall to look. Prince, as his name plate announced, was tall and black and satiny. Amy almost laughed out loud. 'I'll bet you belong to Nicholas,' she said. Oh, this was wonderful! Somehow, she had to convince her mother to let her stay at Sunset Trails!

Charlie paused for another sip of her drink. 'Pretzels, please.' She held out her hand for a bag of pretzels.

'I honestly don't know how you can pack so much junk into your body,' Alex said, as she rummaged in the dark for the pretzels.

'Did Amy get to ride Classy?' Louise asked. 'She sounds like such a great little horse. What colour is a bay?'

'Dark brown, almost black,' Charlie told her. She reached for the bag Alex held out and grabbed a handful of pretzels. 'Mmm, these are good. I like to lick the salt off them before I crunch them! Anybody want some?'

The others shook their heads.

'What about that baby crying?' Jo asked. 'Was it really a tree branch?'

'I'm just telling you the story the way she told it to us,' Charlie said. 'Quit trying to get me ahead of myself. But I can tell you that when Amy got to the part about the crying, she sort of stumbled over her words, almost as if she could hear the crying all over again.'

Five

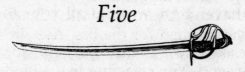

'Stop crunching those pretzels and go on,' Alex complained. 'You are the most hopeless storyteller.'

'I'm just keeping you in suspense,' Charlie laughed. 'That's what good storytellers do.'

'I'm in suspense about Nicholas,' Jo said. 'It sounds as though he looks something like Stephen . . .'

Charlie choked on a pretzel. '*Josephine*,' she spluttered. 'You have gone completely crackers! Stephen Piggott is such a nobody!'

Jo hated to be called Josephine. She flicked sand at Charlie.

'Ugh!' Charlie brushed the sand off her sleeping bag. 'Now you've done it! Everything will feel gritty all night – gritty chocolate, gritty chips, gritty pretzels . . . thanks a lot!'

'I didn't laugh at you when you liked that science geek, Jesse,' Jo flared.

'Well, at least Jesse has some intelligence. Stephen is just a big pile of bones who looks good in riding boots,' Charlie snorted. 'You haven't known him all your life like I have.'

'Please stop,' Louise begged. 'Jo, don't throw sand. You're acting like a kindergarten kid. And Charlie, stop teasing. You can't tell the story and tease Jo at the same time!'

'All right,' Charlie sighed. 'The next break in the story will be for toasted marshmallows!'

'And I promise not to mention Stephen's name again, if it bugs you so much . . .' Jo agreed. 'I wonder what he's doing right now?'

'JO!' they all shouted.

'I'd still like to know what Amy and her mum almost hit with their car,' Alex said. 'Was it really a moose? Why was Nicholas so sure it wasn't a horse?'

'That's what Amy wanted to know, too,' Charlie nodded. 'So the next morning, she got up early to ask him.' Charlie scrunched up her empty pretzel bag and leaned forward so the firelight lit her face as she told her story. Charlie's dark eyes glowed with mystery as she looked at her three friends.

They leaned forward to listen as she began to speak.

Amy ran out of the bunkhouse, eager to have a look around before her mother got up. The riding camp lay peaceful in the dawn light, and right in front of her was the large barn and a riding ring with rail fences.

A girl came out of the barn and waved. She wore baggy overalls and rubber boots. As she came closer, Amy saw that her thick, curly hair was pulled back in a ponytail. She had round, rosy cheeks and a wide smile.

'I'm Caroline,' she said. 'I got here late last night. It took us hours because of the storm! It was pitch dark when we finally pulled in, so I had no idea what the place looked like. It's great, isn't it?'

'Great,' Amy agreed. 'Where *is* everyone?'

'You mean Nicholas and his mother? They've already fed and watered the horses, mucked out the stalls and gone for a ride.' Caroline turned her bright eyes on Amy. 'I've been waiting for months to get here. We had Nicholas Campbell for a one-day clinic at our pony club, and he was fabulous!'

'He looks like a film star,' Amy laughed. 'It's nice to know that he can ride, too!'

'See for yourself. Here he comes.'

Amy swung around to watch two riders coming up the lane. She felt her breath draw in with a gasp.

'What's wrong?' Caroline's alert eyes caught the expression on Amy's face.

'It's just . . . what a horse!' Amy's breath returned. For a second, with the sun behind them, the tall black horse and the tall rider galloping towards her looked exactly like the vision on the quarry road the instant before their car spun out of control.

Caroline nodded. 'Prince is a fabulous horse. But Nicholas is the only one who can manage him. We won't get to ride him.'

'Too bad,' Amy murmured as Nicholas and his mother rode up to the barn.

Sheila Campbell slid from the back of her grey mare and looped the reins expertly over her hand. 'Nicholas and I rode down to look at your car,' she told Amy. 'You and your mother were very lucky that you didn't go right over the edge. That quarry pit really should be fenced off!'

Nicholas had dismounted and was leading Prince away.

'Can you two can give Nicholas a hand with the horses?' Sheila Campbell handed her reins to Amy. 'I should go up to the house and call the garage in North Chadwick about your car.'

'Can we!' Caroline shared a delighted glance with Amy. They led Sheila Campbell's horse into the shady barn and fastened her to the crossties.

A lively dark head with a white blaze down its nose poked over the boards to watch them.

'This is Classy,' Amy ran over to her stall. 'Isn't she beautiful? She stroked Classy's nose and scratched her forehead. Classy bobbed her head in delight.

Nicholas came up behind them. 'She's the best dressage horse we have,' he said, 'but she hasn't been ridden since an accident to her right leg.' He reached over to scratch under Classy's mane. 'I'm a bit worried that her whole right side is getting stiff from lack of exercise, but I don't want to put too much weight on her.' He smiled down at Amy. 'I thought you might be light enough to ride her.'

'I'd love to!'

'Good, we'll try it out later.' Nicholas gave Classy a quick pat and strode away. Amy stood gazing at Classy. Her own right leg had been broken in the car accident, and she remembered the months of exercise to get it back in shape. 'We'll make a good team,' she whispered.

'You're so lucky,' Caroline came over to lean on the stall.

'This is the first time in my life I'm happy to be small,' Amy laughed. 'I guess sometimes it's good to be a shrimp.'

Classy bared her teeth and whinnied, as if to agree with her.

'Can you believe it?' Amy's mother stormed into the bunkhouse an hour later. 'There are only going to be four campers at this place for the whole month of August. I can't leave you at Sunset Trails. It's not a real riding camp at all!'

Amy took a deep breath, and tried to keep her voice calm. 'Yes it is. Mrs Campbell explained that they didn't want to take on too many riding students the first year – Nicholas is training for the horse-riding Grand Prix . . .'

'They probably couldn't get any other campers!' Amy's mother said in disgust. 'Look at my jeans. She didn't even *wash* them last night – just threw them in the dryer. They're still covered in mud.'

Amy bit her tongue to keep from pointing out that Sheila Campbell had more important things to do than wash people's clothes. Instead, she stuck to horses and riding.

'Mrs Campbell and Nicholas are the best showjumping and dressage teachers in New England,' Amy said. 'Sunset Trails will be famous someday.'

'I just don't feel right leaving you in such a . . . shockingly run down place.'

'The barn isn't run down,' Amy insisted. 'And I'm going to ride Classy – the best horse! Nicholas says I'm the only one light enough to ride her. Oh, please, Mum,' she begged. 'Let me stay. I love it here.'

'You love it now, but what if you change your mind, and I have to drive all the way back up these mountain roads to get you,' Amy's mother shuddered. 'I'm afraid I've made up my mind, Amy. We're leaving as soon as I can get the car back on the road.'

*   *   *

'Stop a second,' Jo said from the other side of the fire. 'Listen . . .'

They all listened, straining their eyes to see in the blackness outside the circle of fire. It was no longer possible to see where the beach ended and the water's edge began. All they could hear was the soft lapping of the waves on the shore.

'What is it?' Louise whispered.

'I thought I heard something, out there' Jo whispered back.

'Did it sound like a lake monster slithering up?' Charlie said in a low, scary voice.

'LAKE MONSTER!' Louise screamed, 'WHERE?'

'Please, Louise, I can't hear,' Jo said. 'Listen! there it is again.'

There was the sound of distant splashing, and then a cry.

'Someone else fell into the lake,' Louise gasped.

'Oh, that's just goofy Stephen Piggott and his friends doing cannonballs off his dock,' Charlie said. 'They probably saw our fire and they're trying to show off.'

Now they heard the sound of laughter more clearly.

'They sound so close,' Jo said.

'Don't worry, they're far away. On a still night like this you can hear people on the other side of the lake,' said Charlie.

'I wasn't worried.' Jo said. 'I'd just like to get even with Stephen for laughing at me. I'd like to make him feel as stupid as I did when I fell off that horse.'

'You're making too much out of this,' Alex said. She threw some more sticks on the fire. 'Go on, Charlie. Take us back to Sunset Trails. How did Amy convince her mother to let her stay?'

'She didn't,' Charlie said with a shrug.

Six

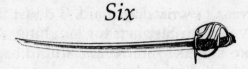

'If everyone is finished hearing weird noises,' Charlie said, 'I'll go on.' She looked pointedly at Jo, who was still gazing in the direction of Stephen's cottage.

'Build up the fire a little,' Louise told Alex. 'It's spooky out here. Why is it so dark all of a sudden?'

'The moon is behind the clouds,' Alex said, leaning forward to lay some fresh wood carefully on the camp-fire. The fire was the one bright spot in the surrounding darkness. It lit Alex's face and reddish gold curls, but left the rest of them in shadow.

As the flames crackled and danced, the circle of light spread. Charlie's voice drew them back into the story. 'Let me tell you what happened. Amy didn't convince her mother . . . something else did.'

Charlie described the scene at the Sunset

Trails Riding Camp, sketching pictures in the air with her words as she spoke.

'I promise I won't change my mind,' Amy shouted. Her mother was being so unfair! It was no use trying to stay calm and reason with her.

Just then, there was the loud honking of a truck horn outside. Amy and her mother hurried to the bunkhouse door, in time to see a truck, towing a fancy horse box, pull up in front of the barn. Two people climbed out.

One was a girl, Amy's age. She must be the third camper, Amy thought. Even from the bunkhouse porch she could see the girl's disapproving stare as she looked around the Sunset Trails camp.

The other passenger was a woman.

Suddenly, Amy's mother clutched her arm. 'I know *her* – she's Maggie Mitchell, my old college roommate. And that tall girl must be her daughter. Come on!' She grabbed Amy's hand and dragged her towards the truck.

While their mothers greeted each other warmly, the new girl examined Amy through designer sunglasses. Victoria had short dark hair, arched eyebrows and a pouty mouth. 'I don't know, Mother,' she drawled, 'I'm not sure this is my kind of . . .'

All at once her voice trailed off into stunned silence. Nicholas and Caroline had just appeared around the corner of the horse box and Nicholas had turned the full force of his smile on Victoria.

She looked like a person who had been struck by lightning, Amy thought. Victoria peeled off her sunglasses and stared at him.

'This is my son, Nicholas,' Sheila introduced him. 'He's competing in the Grand Prix riding event in Boston next month, but he'll have some time to do schooling classes with the campers as well.'

Amy thought she could see Victoria's knees wobbling.

'What were you saying, dear?' Victoria's mother asked.

'Oh. Those riding classes sound . . . brilliant,' Victoria stammered.

Amy suspected there would be no more problems with Victoria wanting to leave. Sure enough, Victoria's horse, Marvel, was soon unloaded from the horse-box. Marvel was an elegant chestnut pony with a bored expression that matched Victoria's perfectly!

Amy could not resist sharing a grin with Caroline as they led him away to the stable.

'Well,' her mother sighed. 'If Maggie Mitchell thinks it's all right for Victoria to stay, I suppose you can too. I'll feel better knowing you have a friend here.'

'I'm going to love it,' Amy promised. If she had a friend, she thought, it certainly wouldn't be Victoria.

Her opinion of Victoria was strengthened when they walked into Caroline's bunkhouse a few minutes later. 'What a dump,' Victoria announced as she flung her expensive bag on the bed. 'Who's sleeping in here?'

'Oh, you can have the *dump* all to yourself, if you like,' Caroline said quickly. 'I'll bunk in with Amy.' She winked at Amy, and grinned.

'Perfect,' Amy nodded. She would rather sleep with a tarantula than Victoria, any day.

'What about the other camper?' Victoria asked. 'Maybe I'll get stuck with her.'

'She's a he,' Caroline said. 'According to Nicholas, his name is John.'

John Cunningham arrived while Amy was

watching the tow truck pull her mother's car on to the road. When they got back to Sunset Trails, John was trying to dodge out of the way of the horses, while his parents hovered nervously. He looked unhappy and out of place.

Caroline was trying to be polite in her nice, friendly way, and Victoria looked aloof.

After hurried introductions, Amy's mother climbed into her little car. 'I'll call as soon as I get home.' She clutched the steering wheel and squinted up at Amy through the car window.

'Don't worry, I'll be fine.' Amy felt an enormous sense of relief as she waved good-bye and watched her mum drive off through the Sunset Trail gates. Now riding camp could really begin.

John Cunningham sat at dinner, twirling his spaghetti round and round on his fork. 'My parents thought riding camp would toughen me up. Why can't you get tough playing chess and video games?'

'It's not the *riding* that bothers me,' Victoria said haughtily. 'But they honestly expect us to muck out stalls and shovel manure. Can you imagine? And this place is such a dump!' She shoved the pasta on her plate to one side, and helped herself to more salad.

Amy and Caroline didn't dare look at each other, for fear they would burst out laughing. They were saved by Nicholas, who came in with a plate of chocolate chip cookies and some announcements.

'The first announcement is that we've decided to start a Sunset Trails tradition,' he said. 'Every night, when the weather is good, we'll meet at the fire pit near the house for a camp-fire. It will be the last activity of the day. We'll have hot chocolate, toasted marshmallows, cookies, and songs.'

John's glum face lit up. 'I love fires,' he said in an excited voice.

Victoria tossed her head as if to say that she was beyond such baby things as camp-fires, but if Nicholas thought it was a good idea, she'd go along with it.

'The second announcement concerns riding,' Nicholas went on. 'There's a one-day event down at Pine Meadows next week,' he announced. 'We'll start training for it tomorrow.'

Victoria puffed up like a preening pigeon. 'I got a first in show-jumping last month at our club,' she announced. 'So you can enter me in that event.'

'My mother and I will assess how you all ride in the morning,' Nicholas smiled round at them. Amy suddenly remembered a question she had wanted to ask him earlier.

'You said the old quarry road was abandoned years ago,' she said. 'Why was it abandoned?'

The smile left Nicholas's eyes. 'The quarry was mined out, I suppose.'

'Are you sure there are no other farms along the road? I'm positive it was a horse we saw last night.'

'You have an overactive imagination,' Nicholas laughed nervously. 'I'm sure it was a moose that ran in front of your car.'

'It *looked* like a horse,' Amy said. 'A black horse, with a rider . . .'

Now Nicholas looked angry. His face was flushed bright red. 'You're imagining things,' he said again. 'Don't spread stories like that!' He slammed down the plate and strode back into the kitchen.

Amy sat, stunned. What was the matter with Nicholas? He had seemed so different before . . . so nice.

'You were positively rude,' Victoria hissed.

'You're not going to get along very well here with manners like that.'

'Who was it called this camp a dump?' Caroline murmured.

'Well, I didn't say it to their faces,' Victoria shot back. She got up from the table and flounced over to a couch on the other side of the room with a magazine.

'Oh, this is all we need,' John said miserably. 'Fights. I hate fights. I'm going to my bunkhouse.' He shoved his glasses up his nose and stomped out.

'I didn't mean to be rude to Nicholas.' Amy protested. 'I don't understand why he got so mad!'

There was silence in the dining-room. From the kitchen, Amy and Caroline could hear the clatter of dishes and a low, urgent conversation between Sheila Campbell and Nicholas.

Caroline scraped back her chair. 'I'm going to see if I can help with the dishes,' she announced. 'Are you done with your spaghetti?' she called to Victoria.

'I never eat pasta,' Victoria said loudly. 'It goes straight to your hips.'

'I'll come and help.' Amy picked up her plate and glass.

As they went through the swinging doors to the kitchen, Caroline chuckled. 'I hope Victoria chokes on the three chocolate chip cookies she's got hidden in her pocket,' she whispered.

Later, as they sat around the flickering Sunset Trails camp-fire, Caroline turned to Amy. 'You know, John was right about fighting,' she said quietly. 'I've been saving all my money since I was eight to come to a camp like this. I don't want it wrecked with people getting upset. Please, Amy?'

Amy looked back at her worried face. 'I want to concentrate on riding as much as you do,' she told Caroline. 'But I just wish I knew why Nicholas got so upset when I mentioned the horse on the road. It's weird – he's almost like two people.' She threw a stick into the fire and watched it blaze up.

Back in their bunkhouse, it took a long time for Amy to fall asleep. Tonight, the shutters were open and the night sounds came through the screen. Branches rustled, crickets sang, and from the barn she heard the occasional whinny from one of the horses.

She tried to think about riding, about

Classy's long flowing mane and tail, her glossy coat, her bright, mischievous look.

She wouldn't think about the black horse in the storm, or the quarry pit, or the dark, lonely road in the rain. She wouldn't think about Nicholas's angry face at dinner.

Tomorrow she would ride Classy. Tomorrow she would have a chance to show what she could do after six months of riding lessons at home . . .

At last Amy's eyes closed and she drifted off.

The drumming hoofbeats woke her from a deep sleep. They beat in a steady rhythm, like the beating of her heart, *thump-a-lump, thump-a-lump*. She heard them like a pressure in her eardrums at first. Then the pounding grew louder and she knew it was a horse.

Amy lay rigid in her bed. Now the hoofbeats were closer, coming straight for the bunkhouse. Nearer and nearer, until she was sure she heard them thunder over the roof. Amy smelled smoke again, burning her nostrils.

She sat bolt upright. Couldn't Caroline hear it? The horse was galloping back towards the bunkhouse again – in another minute it would kick down the bunkhouse walls!

'Caroline!' she screamed, but there was no sign that Caroline heard anything. The thundering hoofbeats filled Amy's brain – there was no time to wake her – she had to escape!

Amy ran to the screen door. The night was pitch-black. Now she could hear the jingle of harness, and the terrible hoofbeats were so loud they seemed to explode in her head!

Her heart raced with terror. She had never been afraid of horses, but this horse meant to harm her. She tore open the screen door and ran out on to the porch.

Too late. In a split second, Amy saw a swirl of darker black motion against the dark night, smelled bitter, acrid smoke, and felt the heat of a powerful onrushing animal. It was so close it seemed to throw her body to one side as it soared into the air.

Amy fell heavily against the porch railing. With a screech of rusty nails, the railing collapsed under her weight and she pitched into the darkness.

As she fell she had a vision of an immense black horse leaping on to the roof. On its back was a hooded rider.

Seven

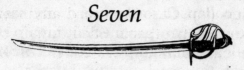

When Amy's head stopped swimming, everything was quiet. She was lying in the prickly, dew-soaked bushes with one leg pinned under the broken porch rail.

Shuddering with cold, Amy sat up and heaved the rail to one side. Her leg throbbed and her head ached from the fall. She managed to limp up the steps and back through the bunkhouse door.

Caroline was still snoring blissfully.

Amy crept into bed and hugged the quilt up tight round her neck. It took her long moments to stop shivering. In her mind she could still hear the galloping horse and feel how close she had been to getting trampled under its great hooves. She tossed and turned in her narrow bed, and finally fell into a deep sleep just as the sun was rising.

Caroline's sudden scream woke her. 'Hey!

What happened out here?' Caroline's round, surprised face appeared at the door. She was already dressed in her riding clothes. 'The porch collapsed in the night,' she said.

'I know,' Amy groaned, sitting up slowly. She felt stiff and groggy. 'The rail broke, and I fell off the porch into the bushes.'

'What were you doing out there in the middle of the night?' Caroline bustled over to the bed.

'I heard a horse,' Amy said. 'It sounded like it was galloping right over the roof, and when I went out on the porch it almost rode me down. It was big, and black . . . like the horse our car almost hit . . . like Prince.'

Caroline stared at her. 'I didn't hear anything. You must have had a nightmare. Here, let me help you up.'

Amy stood on wobbly legs. 'There's something else. When the horse came, the room seemed full of smoke.'

'Maybe it was the smoke from our campfire.' Caroline said. 'I don't smell anything now.' She shook her head and her brown ponytail bounced from side to side. 'Sometimes it's hard to sleep in a new place. Why don't you stay here and rest this morning?'

'Are you kidding?' Amy gave herself a brisk shake and reached for her riding clothes. 'Miss the first day of lessons? Never!'

Victoria had already arrived when they got to the stables. She was wearing light tan riding pants and leather boots.

'You might want to wear something less dressy for mucking out the stables,' Sheila Campbell suggested. She was heaving fork-fuls of dirty straw from the stalls into a wheelbarrow.

'These are the only kind of clothes I brought,' Victoria said haughtily. 'Mother and I thought I would be riding, not mucking out horse manure!'

Sheila stopped and leaned on her fork. She wiped her forehead on the sleeve of her shirt. 'Looking after horses *is* part of riding,' she said. 'Here you'll learn to be completely responsible for your horse, for his feeding, grooming, and mucking out. If you want to do that in those riding pants, that's fine. If you want to borrow some jeans, I probably have some that you could wear.' She handed Victoria a pitchfork. 'Here. Why don't you put some clean straw in that stall I just finished.'

Amy and Caroline watched Victoria's face go scarlet as she listened to this speech. She glared at the two of them and grabbed the fork from Sheila.

'You two are late,' Sheila said briefly. 'We need everybody in the barn by six. Amy, go and wake up John,' she ordered. 'Tell him he'd better be here in five minutes if he wants breakfast.'

On the way from the barn to John's bunkhouse, Amy saw Nicholas circling the riding ring on Prince. She stopped for a second to watch. Prince came galloping towards her and soared over a jump as if it were not even there. Amy's mind flew back to her nightmare of a leaping black horse. She shook her head to get rid of the vision and hurried on.

'John,' she roared from the bottom of the bunkhouse steps, 'come on. You're late!' The only way to cope with John, she had decided, was to treat him like a little brother, even though they were the same age.

John came scrambling out of the front door, his shirt buttoned crookedly and his rubber boots on the wrong feet. 'How can I be late when I haven't had breakfast and it's only seven o'clock!' he grumbled to himself.

He stopped abruptly when he saw her. 'Oh, hello, Amy.'

'The horses eat before we do,' Amy told him. 'We're supposed to feed them and work for an hour in the stables before breakfast.'

'Are you joking?' John croaked. 'This horse business is insane,' He stumbled down the front steps and ran to catch up to her. 'At computer camp last year we didn't even *get up* until eight.'

After chores and breakfast they gathered in the stable for their first lesson. 'There's a pail of carrots over there,' Sheila Campbell told Amy. 'Offer some to Classy while you're getting her lead rope on. She can be a difficult horse, but just show her you mean business.'

Amy stuck a carrot down the top of her boot, another under her arm, and held a third in her hand. As she went into Classy's stall the little mare looked interested in the carrot held flat on Amy's outstretched palm. Amy spoke quietly and gently to her and waited until the carrot had been crunched between strong yellow teeth before reaching up with the lead rope.

Classy backed away, snorting. 'There's another carrot for you,' Amy said, coming close and turning so Classy could smell the carrot under her arm. 'See if you can find it.'

While Classy was nosing round her shirt, Amy snapped the lead rope on her halter and led her out to the crossties. 'So you like to play games, do you?' Amy said. 'Well there's another carrot somewhere. Try and find it while I get your saddle and bridle on.'

'That's good,' Sheila said, watching her do up the saddle girth round Classy's belly as the horse crunched the final carrot. 'I don't think you'll have any trouble with her.'

For the first lesson they just rode round the ring, getting the feel of their mounts, trying out the different gaits. 'Classy likes to lead,' Sheila called, 'Amy should go first.'

Amy could hear Victoria's snort of protest as she walked Classy past Marvel. Victoria didn't like being second at anything!

But the minute Classy began to trot, Amy forgot Victoria. She felt as though she were riding in a dream. The little bay mare responded to the slightest signal from her legs, or her hands. She seemed to float round the ring, to sense Amy's wishes.

'That's fine,' she heard Sheila call. 'Now we'll work one at a time. Victoria, you go first.'

Amy slipped off Classy's back to watch Victoria ride. Victoria's horse, Marvel, was a showy, good-natured pony, there was no doubt. But he had none of Classy's *class*.

It was clear in the next few days that Victoria knew the difference too. 'Anybody could look good on that horse,' she muttered.

That morning, Classy tried to get ahead of Marvel, and nipped his flank. Victoria lost her temper. 'You keep your horse away from mine,' she said, turning with a furious glance at Amy.

Nicholas Campbell tried to play down the competition between the Sunset Trails riders. 'This is a team effort,' he told them. 'We need winners at all levels to show what this camp can do.'

'I won't win anything,' John groaned. He had trouble just keeping Mustard, his plump Welsh pony, going in the right direction.

'You'll be in the 'Future Champions' level,'

Nicholas told him. 'A win there is just as important as at any level.'

'You mean I'm in the baby class,' John groaned. 'Oh, I wish I was at computer camp.'

But Caroline and Amy were in heaven. Caroline's favourite event was showjumping. 'I think Joker has a good chance for a ribbon,' she said as she brushed down the tall black gelding after a long training session. 'And you and Classy will do really well in dressage.'

'I'd love to win a ribbon.' Amy sighed blissfully. 'That would prove to my mother that I was serious about riding.'

'Don't count on winning,' Victoria said. 'Dressage is my event.' Her normally pretty face was set in a sulky scowl. When the others straggled up to the house for lunch, Victoria stayed behind.

They were just starting on hamburgers, cooked by Nicholas on the fire-pit grill, when a screech sounded from the stables.

'It's Victoria,' Caroline said. 'Something's happened.'

They raced to the stables, leaving the rest of the hamburgers burning.

'My leg!' Victoria moaned, from a heap

of straw where she lay crumpled. 'Classy . . . kicked me.' Her face was twisted with pain, and when she stood up there was a black smudge on the shin of her riding pants. 'That horse is vicious,' Victoria cried through gritted teeth. 'I was just trying to feed her a carrot . . .'

'Can you put any weight on your leg?' Nicholas asked.

Victoria gave a tearful nod and allowed Nicholas to help her into a standing position. By the time they reached the house, Victoria was loudly proclaiming that she was going to complain to her mother unless Classy was removed.

Sheila looked terribly worried. Classy had a history of bad behaviour, Amy knew. But since she'd been riding her, Classy had been a lamb. Sometimes she was a little frisky, but she had never tried to bite or kick . . . except for the occasional nip at Marvel.

'Let's take a look at your shin,' Nicholas said. He lowered Victoria into the armchair beside the fireplace.

Victoria made a huge production of painfully removing her left boot and trying to roll up the leg of her riding pants. 'I can't,' she gasped, 'It's too tight. My leg must be swelling.'

'Should we get a doctor?' Nicholas asked his mother.

'Maybe,' Sheila said. 'Let's wait and see how she is in an hour or so. In the meantime, I'm calling Bradley.' She strode to the phone.

'The horse dealer?' Nicholas sounded shocked.

'I can't have a dangerous horse at the camp,' Sheila shook her head. 'There is too much at stake . . . I'm going to sell her.'

'Before the event at Pine Meadows?'

'If possible,' Sheila nodded grimly. She turned to Amy with the phone in her hand. 'I'm sorry, Amy, but I can't take a chance.'

'I don't believe it,' Louise interrupted the story. 'Victoria is faking!'

'Poor Amy,' Jo exclaimed. 'First that awful dream about the horse, and now this!'

'Do you think it *was* just a dream?' Alex said thoughtfully. 'She and her mum almost hit a horse on the road, and then a huge black horse wakes her up out of a sound sleep. I think there's something weird going on at that camp. Am I right, Charlie?'

Charlie was pawing through the food bag with her flashlight in one hand. 'I'm trying to find the marshmallows,' she said. 'If you guys are going to keep interrupting me, we might as well eat.'

Eight

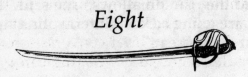

'I'll never interrupt again,' Louise promised. 'Please go on.'

'The fire is burning too hot to toast marsh-mallows anyway,' Alex told Charlie. 'All you'll get is cinders on sticks.'

'Wait till it burns down to nice hot embers,' Jo agreed. 'Then they'll be per-fect. Golden brown on the outside, nice and gooey on the inside . . .'

'All right,' Charlie grumbled. 'Pass me a couple of cookies to tide me over, and I'll go on.'

They waited while Charlie munched up six fudge cookies, wiped the crumbs off her hands, and started to speak.

Victoria looked smug, as Sheila Campbell picked up the phone and put in her call to the horse dealer.

Amy stared at Caroline in despair. It seemed so unfair. All the work she had put in learning the dressage routine on Classy was wasted. She sat numbly listening to Sheila Campbell's brief conversation.

'Bradley's not sure when he can get out here,' Sheila told Nicholas, as she hung up the phone. 'It might be a couple of days.'

She had two days, Amy thought, two days to think of a way to keep Classy.

That night, after camp-fire, when everything was dark, Amy stole out of the bunkhouse. Nicholas had repaired the railing so it was now smooth and new under her hand as she felt her way down the steps.

As soon as she was far enough from the bunkhouses, Amy switched on her flashlight so she could see her way to the barn. The air was still. There was a feeling of another summer storm coming.

Amy opened the big barn door and stepped into the warm, horse-fragrant stable. She heard Prince whinny in the darkness and stomp around in his stall.

Classy's stall was next to his.

'It's me,' Amy told Classy, holding out a carrot on her outstretched palm. Classy's

63

soft muzzle sniffed the carrot, then gently lifted it from her hand. Then she nuzzled Amy's arm, searching for another carrot.

Amy was not afraid. She reached up under Classy's mane and stroked her warm neck, then laid her head along Classy's cheek. 'I don't believe you kicked Victoria,' she murmured. 'But if you did, I'm sure you had a good reason. I often feel like kicking her myself.'

Somehow, Amy thought, she had to keep Sheila from selling Classy. She and the little bay mare were a team. She knew daily riding was helping Classy's stiff right leg, and Classy would help her become a good rider. They would win ribbons, and her mother would finally understand she was serious about riding.

There might be a chance to keep her if the horse dealer didn't come until after the show at Pine Meadows. *If* Sheila let her ride Classy, and *if* Classy won a medal in dressage . . . Amy felt tears in her eyes. There were too many ifs.

A few minutes later, the storm began with a rush of rain. It pounded on the metal roof of the barn, drowning out Amy's thoughts. Classy stayed calm.

'Good girl,' Amy said, stroking her soft muzzle. This was no vicious, excitable horse! But Prince, in the next stall, began to whinny in excitement. A crack of thunder made him rear and snort in fear. Amy could hear his hoofs pound against the thick wooden wall between the stalls until she was afraid he would kick it to pieces.

And now . . . Amy clutched herself in horror . . . she smelled smoke. She was suddenly back in her nightmare with the pounding hooves and the smoky smell surrounding her.

Amy's knees gave way and she crouched at the back of Classy's stall, shivering with fear.

She felt a soft pressure on her head. She reached up in terror, but found only a soft inquisitive nose. Classy had come over to nuzzle her neck. That gave her courage.

She shone the flashlight around the stall to see where the smoky smell might be coming from. At the base of the outside wall was a thick black beam. It looked, in this light, like charred wood.

Amy bent closer and rubbed her finger along the foundation beam. There was a black smudge on her finger. At some time there must have been a fire that had scorched these foundation beams, but not burned through.

Amy straightened up. Had something moved out there in the dark? An eerie feeling crawled up her spine.

'Hello?' Amy called. 'Is someone there?'

Footsteps rustled in the straw. Nicholas stepped out of the shadows. He leaned on his arms on the top of Classy's stall and looked at Amy. 'What are you doing here?'

'I came to say goodbye to Classy,' Amy gulped. 'In case she gets sold tomorrow.'

Nicholas said nothing. He reached over to the next stall. 'Easy boy,' he told Prince. The big horse was still stomping and snorting, but he quieted at Nicholas's touch.

'Nicholas?' Amy said. 'Was there ever a fire in this barn? I found some charred beams along the foundation wall. And I wondered . . . because sometimes I seem to smell smoke . . . at night.'

There was silence for a moment. 'What kind of nonsense are you making up now?' Nicholas finally asked in a low voice.

'I'm not making anything up!' Amy stood straighter. 'I saw a horse on the road. I've heard a horse galloping in the night, and I smell smoke. And now I find these burned beams in the barn. Look . . . they're real!' She shone her flashlight beam at the base of Classy's stall.

Nicholas seemed about to blurt something out, then got control of himself. 'You're right,' he said. 'Something did happen in this barn, a long time ago.' There were lines of tension round his handsome mouth.

Amy held her breath, hoping he would go on.

'But it has nothing to do with Sunset Trails,' Nicholas said. 'It was all in the past. I'll make a deal with you,' he glanced in her direction. 'You don't want Classy to get sold, right?'

Amy shook her head. 'Of course not!'

'We all know that Classy isn't a dangerous horse,' Nicholas went on. 'But Victoria's mother is very powerful in riding circles, and if Victoria complains, a word from her could ruin Sunset Trails. That's why mother is selling Classy.'

Amy had suspected something like that.

'But I'll stop Victoria from complaining,' Nicholas promised, 'if you'll stop spreading stories about the camp.' Nicholas reached his long arm over the stall partition. 'Do we have a deal?'

Amy shook his hand, wondering what story from the past could make Nicholas so afraid. 'It's a deal,' she agreed.

'Exercise break,' Charlie announced, jumping up and waving her arms. 'And look at those red-hot embers in the fire. They're absolutely perfect for toasting marshmallows!'

'Exercise didn't last long,' Alex grumbled.

'Well, we can't all be athletic like you,' Charlie retorted. 'Where *are* those marshmallows?

'You're so irritating,' Jo sighed. 'You just get us into a good part and then you get hungry again. You're a bottomless pit.'

'I'm glad we're taking a break.' Louise shivered. She was feeling round in the dark for her pointed marshmallow-toasting stick. 'I felt as if I was right in that barn, smelling the smoke, hearing things . . .' Of all of them, Louise had the best imagination and was the most easily scared.

'Me too. And then Nicholas appeared. There's something about him . . .' Jo said, hugging herself with glee. Jo loved mysterious stories, the scarier the better!

Charlie had stuck a marshmallow on a stick and was toasting it over the glowing embers. She was concentrating fiercely on melting it without having it burst into flames.

'Jo,' Alex suddenly clutched Jo's arm. Her usually calm voice was husky with surprise. 'Look over there. Those two dots of light by the bushes. Is that one of Charlie's tricks?'

'I don't think so,' Jo whispered back. 'They're moving.'

The two glowing dots had multiplied. Now there were six pairs, staring straight at them. The eyeshine was deep amber.

'They're some kind of wild animal . . . that can see in the dark,' Jo whispered. 'Don't say anything to Louise. She'll be sure to think it's Charlie's lake monster.'

'Lake monster? Where?' Charlie swung round violently. The hot, gooey marshmallow, toasted to perfection, flew off her stick. It plopped into the sand, just in front of the pairs of glowing eyes.

As they watched, one of the pairs began to move. There was a white smear in the darkness, a strong, musky odour.

'Don't move,' Alex said quietly. 'And whatever you do, anybody, don't scream or shout.'

The glowing eyes were closing in on the marshmallow.

'What's that terrible smell?' Louise managed to croak. 'Is it . . . the giant snake?'

'Worse.' Alex said. 'Skunks.'

Nine

As the four girls froze motionless around the fire, six skunks moved out into the light. The mother skunk was enormous – black with two white stripes down her back. The five baby skunks were almost full grown. They surrounded their mother while she smacked at the sweet, melted marshmallow.

'What are we going to do?' Jo whispered.

'Flick them another marshmallow,' Alex suggested. 'See if you can get it further away.'

Louise's marshmallow was blazing by now. She pulled it out and blew out the flame, then waved her stick like a fishing rod, trying to send the blackened gob of sugar far into the bushes. Instead, the melted marshmallow sailed through the air and landed right in the middle of Charlie's T-shirt.

The six skunks closed in on Charlie. They

walked flat-footed, like fat little bears. They smelled disgusting.

'Do something,' Charlie moaned. 'The big one is almost in my lap!'

'Just don't provoke them,' Alex hissed. 'She won't spray if she isn't upset.' She picked up the whole bag of uncooked marshmallows. 'Here, skunks,' she said in a soft low voice. 'Here are some nice, plump, unburnt ones.'

One by one, Alex lobbed white marshmallows off into the bushes. The mother skunk gave up trying to climb on Charlie's lap. She waddled off, the young skunks in a perfect row behind her, their tails in the air.

'Whew,' Alex sighed, when the rustling and snuffling in the bushes had died away. 'It's a good thing they didn't spray, or our camp-fire sleepover would have been over right now!'

'You threw away half my marshmallows,' Charlie groaned.

'Too much sugar isn't good for your teeth, anyway.' Alex laughed.

'They've got a lot of nerve, crashing our sleepover,' Charlie said. 'We've had little brothers, mice, bellboys and a big dog crash our sleepovers before, but never skunks!'

'You don't think Stephen and his friends will crash the sleepover, do you?' Jo asked.

'I'll drown them if they try,' Charlie was still trying to get the melted marshmallow out of her T-shirt, and getting it stuck in her silky black hair instead. 'We'll have to take a break in the story while I get unstuck,' she laughed. 'Did anybody bring soap?'

Louise had some in her backpack. The others waited while Charlie sponged off her T-shirt in the lake and dried it with a towel.

'We might have known,' Jo sighed. 'With Charlie telling a story things weren't likely to go smoothly.'

'I want to find out about that horse that Amy heard on the roof,' Louise said.

'. . . And whether she gets to ride Classy in the horse show,' Jo added.

'I'm coming,' Charlie called. 'Just get comfortable and I'll be there in a second.'

The others settled down by the fire. Alex carefully placed some small kindling on the glowing embers to get the fire blazing again. When the fire was crackling and shooting flames into the night sky, she added three big logs.

'All set, she said. 'It will burn for a long time now.'

Charlie plunked back down on the sand. 'Remember, Amy made a deal with Nicholas,' she said. 'But there were only a couple of days before the horse show and Amy was terrified he wouldn't find a way to save Classy before then.'

Charlie's cheerful teasing voice changed again. As the story swept forward, they could hear the tension building in her voice.

By the next afternoon, Nicholas had kept his part of the bargain. Somehow, he convinced Victoria she should ride Classy in the cross-country event. And he had talked his mother into keeping Classy until after the horse show at Pine Meadows.

'Nicholas says if I ride Classy, I might win a ribbon in cross-country,' Victoria crowed. 'Marvel is hopeless in cross-country. As soon as he sees a big field he wants to run away and eat grass.'

It was the night before the show. The evening's camp-fire had been cancelled and all the campers were in the barn, grooming their horses. Manes and tails were neatly braided, coats brushed until they gleamed.

'I'd be afraid to ride a horse that had kicked me,' John said, backing away from Classy. They had all seen Victoria's spectacular bruise by now. Her whole shin was purple.

'You're afraid of your own shadow,' Victoria said cruelly. 'Nicholas says I just have to show her who's boss.' She tossed her head. 'He's been giving me private lessons on Classy.'

Caroline and Amy were tying ribbons into their horses' manes. They glanced quickly at each other, with the ghost of a grin. Nicholas's lessons had been very effective!

The next morning they had to be in the barn by five-thirty. A drizzly, damp day was dawning when Amy and Caroline jolted John out of his bed at five.

'It's too early!' John's brown hair was sticking up in spikes. 'I can't think of one single thing worth getting up for at five o'clock.'

Mustard seemed to have the same idea. When his turn came to get in the horse van, the little horse bucked and twisted and balked with his sturdy legs planted firmly in the muddy soil. He would not get in.

'He's kicking mud all over my clean riding pants,' Victoria screeched. 'Can't somebody do something?'

'You'll have to go without me and Mustard,' John yawned. 'Then I can go back to bed.'

'If we don't leave soon, there's no use *any* of us going,' Nicholas pointed out. 'We have to register at Pine Meadows by eight-thirty. It's already after seven and it takes an hour to get there, at least!'

'You go,' Sheila Campbell spoke with decision. 'Take the girls – their horses are already loaded in the van. I'll stay with John.'

Amy was wedged in the front seat of the truck between Victoria and Caroline.

Nicholas was too advanced to compete at Pine Meadows, but he had been asked to give a jumping demonstration. 'I can't wait to see your demonstration,' Victoria cooed.

Caroline gave a grunt of disgust, and nudged Amy with her elbow.

Behind them, the hired horse van bumped along, with Classy, Marvel, Joker and Prince aboard.

They arrived at Pine Meadows almost too late. But Amy's heart lifted as they unloaded the horses. The yard was a tangle of horse vans, horses and kids in riding gear. Standing there, holding Classy's reins, she wished her mother had come to see her ride.

'The dressage event will be first,' Nicholas looked at the schedule. 'We should get the horses over there. It's the ring to the right. Amy, you should warm up on Classy. You ride first.'

A moment later, Amy looked up in alarm from the back of the Sunset Trails truck. 'I can't find my saddle girth . . . I know I packed it with my other stuff.'

'I don't believe this!' Nicholas said. 'Your event is in a few minutes. You can't ride without a girth!'

Amy glimpsed a little smirk in the corner of Victoria's mouth. She had a good idea what had happened to her girth!

'*I'll* go and get warmed up,' Victoria said, swinging into Marvel's saddle. 'Just in case Amy can't ride and I have to take her place.' She gave Amy a superior smile and rode away.

'I'll go and see if I can borrow a girth,'

Nicholas said through clenched teeth. 'Some-one must have an extra.'

Amy stood miserably, watching Victoria and Caroline warm up their horses. Next to her, a small group of girls were leaning on the fence. One of them pointed at Victoria. 'See that girl on the chestnut pony? She's from the Sunset Trails Riding Camp. You know, the *spooky* one?'

'You wouldn't catch *me* staying up there!' another girl giggled. 'They should have called it Ghost Road Riding Camp, not Sunset Trails.'

Amy turned with a start. 'I'm from Sunset Trails, too.' She stared at the girl who had spoken. 'Why wouldn't you stay at our camp?'

'I guess you're not from around here, or you'd know,' the girl glanced sideways at Amy. 'My grandmother used to tell us about the ghost road that leads to the camp. People disappeared on that road and were never seen again. They say the ghost rider got them.'

'Maybe their bodies ended up in the bottomless pit up there near the camp,' a second girl added. 'But nobody knows.'

Amy felt her knees go weak. 'Does the

ghost rider . . . ride around the camp at night? Does he ride over the roofs . . . ?' she stammered.

The girls turned and stared at her, three pale faces under the brims of their riding helmets. 'I never heard *that*,' the first one shrugged. 'Maybe *that's* why the place is always up for sale . . .'

She didn't finish. At that moment Victoria came galloping up on Marvel, with Caroline behind her. 'We should go – the competition must be starting.'

Caroline reined in her horse and looked curiously from Amy to the three girls and back again. 'Aren't you going to come and watch?' she asked.

'In a minute,' Amy told her. She desperately wanted to ask these girls more questions about the ghost rider.

'Are they from Sunset Trails, too?' the first girl asked, as Caroline and Victoria rode away.

Amy nodded.

'Are you going to tell them about . . . you know?' the second girl asked Amy.

'I want to ask you . . .' Amy started.

But at that moment, Nicholas came rushing towards her, waving a saddle girth he had managed to borrow. 'Come on, run!' he shouted. 'You can still make it!'

Nicholas's appearance had the usual dramatic effect on the three girls leaning on the fence. They stared. 'Is he . . . ?' one of them gasped.

'Yes!' Amy shouted over her shoulder. 'He's from Sunset Trails, too! I'll see you later. I have to go.'

She couldn't tell Caroline about the ghost rider, she realised, as she hurried after Nicholas. She had promised him not to spread stories.

Ten

By the time Amy raced back to the dressage ring, Nicholas was tightening the borrowed girth round Classy's belly.

Victoria was having a panic attack. 'Nicholas, they've changed the dressage ring around!' she shrieked. 'The letters on the fence are all in the wrong places! They can't do that, can they?'

'Don't worry!' Nicholas said firmly. 'The letters are reversed, that's all. Just ride to the end of the ring, and when you turn and salute the judges, imagine you've just walked into the ring back at the camp.'

'That's easy for *you* to say,' Victoria stormed. She threw furious glances at the judges, who were lined up along the fence. 'How dare they change the course. We should complain . . .'

Meanwhile, Amy got into the saddle, tested the length of the stirrups and whispered in

Classy's ear. 'We've got to be perfect, now. I don't want to lose you.'

Classy twitched her ears to the side, to show she was listening. Once in the ring she obeyed all the silent commands sent to her through Amy's hands and legs and body position. She lowered her head and blew happily, showing she was enjoying this work. At the end, Amy knew they had an almost perfect score.

Then it was Victoria's turn. Marvel ambled good-naturedly into the ring. His ears were forward, a sure sign that he was not paying attention. Nicholas had got permission from the judges to call out the course to Victoria. 'At C, track left,' he bellowed from the side-lines, 'H to M, ordinary trot, posting. M to A, change diagonal, ordinary trot, sitting.'

Victoria was a good rider, Amy thought. But Marvel just seemed to clump along. He had none of Classy's eagerness and grace.

Victoria did not look pleased as she rode out of the ring and looked down at Amy. 'My leg was hurting,' she announced. 'And I just couldn't get used to the new order.' She glared at the judges, who were now scribbling on their notepads.

Caroline was the last to ride. Amy crossed

her fingers as Caroline halted, faced the judges, and bowed her head in salute.

'Too bad,' she heard Victoria sniff. 'Caroline always looks so . . . lumpy. Her hair is sticking out in clumps, and her jacket doesn't fit. And those boots . . . !' Caroline's boots were caked with mud from the warm-up ring.

Amy itched to say something, but she thought of Classy and kept quiet. After Victoria rode Classy in the cross-country she would deal with her, but not until then.

The day passed in a blur. After lunch, Nicholas displayed his jumping skill on Prince. He rode the course, soaring over the highest jumps, looking like a young prince himself.

'That's my instructor,' Victoria bragged to the girls lining the fence.

They were the same three girls Amy had talked to at the warm-up ring. 'He's *gorgeous*,' one of them sighed. 'What's his name?'

'Nicholas Campbell. He rides Grand Prix events.' Victoria said proudly. 'His mother owns Sunset Trails.'

'She must be crazy to start a camp up there,' the second girl shook her head. 'Don't they know that old farm is haunted?' She

83

peered over at Amy. 'Did your friend tell you about the ghost rider on the old road?'

Amy held her breath. If Victoria said no, they would spill the whole story. And she would repeat it to Nicholas.

But Victoria just shrugged. 'Oh, sure. Amy said she saw someone riding along the road . . .' Victoria remembered. 'But so what? I don't believe in ghosts. Neither does Nicholas . . .' She turned adoring eyes back to the young man on the powerful black horse who was sailing easily over a five-barred gate.

'My grandmother used to say that you had to be a bit psychic to hear or see the ghost rider,' the third girl put in. 'Not everybody can.'

'A bit weird, you mean,' Victoria scoffed. 'There's no such thing as a ghost.' She flounced away to get Marvel ready for their turn in the ring.

Am I psychic, or am I weird? Amy wondered. Or was it possible that *Prince* could jump as high as the bunkhouse roof? He had just flown over the last jump, a sturdy-looking wall as high as her head.

The jumps were lowered for the beginner's

class. The hardest part, Amy thought, was remembering to jump them in the right order. Poor Caroline got confused and was disqualified for not crossing the starting line.

'You are *such* a loser!' Victoria sneered.

Caroline's normally calm face flushed an angry red. 'You didn't ride a perfect round yourself.' Marvel had knocked the bars off several gates.

'It's my leg,' Victoria tossed her head. 'It just didn't feel right.'

'You still have to ride Classy in the cross-country event,' Amy reminded her. 'I'm sure you'll be great.' She patted Classy's silky nose, and whispered in her ear. 'You have to make Miss know-it-all, big-mouth Victoria look good, do you hear?'

The cross-country was the last event of the day. In a large field, jumps, ditches and rails had been laid out, and, as in the jumping, the riders had to guide their horses through in a certain order. Time counted too.

When it was her turn, Victoria came to take Classy's reins out of Amy's hand. 'She'd better not try anything with me,' Victoria warned, jerking the bit in Classy's mouth.

'Careful . . .' Amy could not help crying out. 'She's got a very soft mouth.'

'Nicholas said to be firm,' Victoria said, and wheeled away on Classy, through the fence and up to the starting block.

Classy's ears were back, a sign she was annoyed. She was capable of running away with Victoria, Amy thought, once she was out in the middle of the cross-country field. Amy crossed her fingers again. 'Come on, Classy,' she said. 'Behave, please behave.' She could see Nicholas watching nervously.

And now Victoria's ride began. It was like watching a horror movie, Amy thought. You knew something terrible was going to happen – you just didn't know when! Classy frisked out of the starting block, trotted to the end of the field, went through the rails, scampered across some logs, a low jump and, finally, came down to the last hurdle.

It was clear that Victoria was struggling to keep control. Classy was prancing nervously, head high.

'Soften your hands as you press with your legs,' Nicholas called out. 'Give to her over the jump.' But he was too far away for Victoria to hear.

Classy approached the last jump at a

bumpy trot, then suddenly, without warning, stopped. Victoria went flying over her neck and landed with a plop in the ditch. It had been raining all day and the ditch was full of muddy water.

They all raced up the field, but Victoria had already staggered to her feet. Her perfect riding outfit was plastered with mud. Her helmet was over one eye. 'That stupid, stupid horse,' she raged. 'You should sell her as soon as you can!'

Amy and Caroline ran to catch Classy who had wandered off with her reins dangling in the mud. Amy was almost crying. She was shocked to hear a snort of laughter burst from Caroline. 'Did you see that?' Caroline laughed. 'Right in the mud! I loved it.'

At the awards ceremony, Victoria sat looking like a thunder cloud, while Amy went up to collect a blue ribbon in dressage, a red in cross-country, and a trophy for best rider in her class. Victoria won the blue ribbon for jumping, Caroline the blue in cross-country.

Victoria clumped away from the ceremony and refused to help loading the van. Out of the corner of her eye, Amy saw her talking to the three local riders.

She came back, narrowing her eyes at Amy, glancing at Nicholas. 'They said to watch out for the ghostly rider,' she told Amy. 'They said to watch out for him on moonless nights, whatever that means!'

'You've been spreading stories. You broke our bargain,' Nicholas whispered furiously. He slammed the door of the van shut. 'Don't expect me to protect Classy any longer.'

'I didn't say anything!' Amy's eyes blazed. 'Everybody who lives around here knows about the ghost rider! Everybody tells stories about Sunset Trails!'

Nicholas turned pale. For a moment he looked almost frightened.

'But don't worry,' Victoria stepped between them and put a hand on Nicholas's arm. 'We don't believe in any of that stuff. At least, *some* of us don't.'

Nicholas was still pale. 'Good for you, Victoria,' he muttered. 'See if you can talk some sense into your friend here.'

'Ooo-h!' Louise said. 'I hate that Victoria.'

'I can imagine how she felt, though,' Jo said. 'She must have hated falling off in front of

Nicholas like that. It's so humiliating. And then when everyone laughs . . . you just want to die. And you want revenge! You want them to feel ridiculous and ashamed . . .'

'Jo, for the love of pizza! You've got to get over it,' Charlie said. 'You don't want to be like Victoria.'

'We all feel stupid sometimes,' Alex agreed.

Jo stared at them across the camp-fire. 'But not in front of . . . in front of someone . . .'

'I keep telling you,' Charlie roared, 'Stephen is nobody you have to impress. He's no Nicholas Campbell – tall, bronzed, handsome.'

'Well, he *is* tall,' Jo said slowly.

'Sure. Tall like a sorry-looking weed,' Charlie laughed.

'And I kind of like the colour of his hair . . .'

'Sludge brown?'

'And his face . . .'

'Narrow, mean little eyes, a big nose and . . .' Charlie threw up her arms. 'I don't want to talk about Stephen Piggott one more second. Anyone want a drink?' She reached for the cooler full of ice and drinks, and dragged it towards the fire.

Before she could open it something sprang

out from under the cooler, and, dazzled by the light, gave an enormous hop – right into the fire pit.

Charlie leaped to her feet. 'It's Grog!' she screamed. 'He'll be burned alive!'

Alex moved swiftly. She snatched up the pail of water and threw it on the fire, soaking Louise's sleeping bag, spattering Charlie and Jo.

'Where's Grog?' Charlie cried.

'There!' Louise gasped. The biggest bull-frog they had ever seen hopped out of the smoke and flames. It sat gasping on the sand, a bit charred, but still breathing.

'Meet Grog, the oldest frog in the lake.' Charlie bent over him anxiously. 'We see him every summer. He likes to hide under our boats and I guess he thought the cooler would be a nice shelter for the night.'

'Get him to go back in the water,' Louise said. 'He still looks kind of hot.'

Alex shooed Grog down the beach towards the lake. They heard a loud plop, and he was gone.

'I hope he's okay,' Jo sighed. 'You seem to have a lot of wildlife around here, Charlie. Skunks, bullfrogs . . . is there anything else we're likely to squish in our sleep?'

Eleven

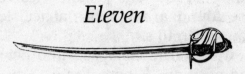

'I thought this would be a nice quiet place to tell a ghost story,' Charlie said, her dark eyes dancing. 'It's not turning out that way.'

Louise was trying to wring the water out of her sleeping bag. Alex was repairing the drenched fire. It was sending up clouds of smoke, making everyone choke.

'It's not your fault, Charlie,' Jo coughed. 'It's a great story. What happened when they got back to Sunset Trails after the horse show?'

'Once Alex gets the fire going again, I'll tell you,' Charlie promised. 'We need some paper to burn.'

'Here,' Jo handed her the almost empty box of snack crackers. 'Eat the rest of these, and burn the box.'

Charlie stuffed the crackers in her mouth and threw the empty cardboard box on the sputtering fire. It blazed up like a torch, and Alex added small sticks, and then larger ones, until the fire was cheerfully crackling again. The smoke cleared and Louise found a dry spot on her sleeping bag on which to sit.

'Now,' Charlie collapsed into her cross-legged position. 'Where was I?'

The four girls settled comfortably around the fire, with the dark at their backs, while Charlie's voice took them back to the scene at the Sunset Trails Riding Camp.

As she fed and watered Classy for the night, Amy thought about the ghostly rider stories. It was so strange. She had seen and heard a rider who exactly matched the stories people told about Sunset Trails.

So, either the story was true, and there *was* a ghost, or someone, for some reason, was trying to make her believe it was true. But *why*? Her mind went round and round in circles. She wished she had someone to talk to about the ghost, but Caroline didn't want to know, and Victoria didn't believe. And as for Nicholas . . . !

Amy looked up and saw John. He was forking fresh straw into Mustard's stall.

He'd been very quiet since the girls had come back from Pine Meadows.

'John,' Amy whispered, tugging at his elbow, 'I need your help tomorrow morning.'

'Leave me alone,' he muttered.

'You said you were good at solving puzzles.'

John stopped pitching straw. He turned and looked at her. 'How early do I have to get up for this?'

'Not too early, I'll tell you about it at campfire tonight,' Amy said. 'Sit beside me.'

The next morning, John was waiting at the barn when Amy arrived in the first light of dawn. The mist was curling up from the grass as they saddled Mustard and Classy and went out through the Sunset Trails gates.

'Okay, where's this ghost road?' John asked.

'It's down here, past the fork,' Amy said. 'There's a big pit where Mum and I had our accident. I want to find out why our car went off the road, and explore the place in the daylight.'

They turned at the fork and crossed the bridge. Their horses' hoofs making hollow clopping sounds on the stones.

The old road wound down through the trees. Scraps of fog were caught in the treetops. It was hard to see anything but the road ahead.

When John spoke, his voice sounded loud and echoey. 'I like this kind of riding. It's better than going round and round in circles in that ring.'

Amy wanted to tell him to hush . . . she was listening. But all she heard was the squawk of ravens, circling high above them. They must be looking for something to eat, she thought. Something that might have fallen into the pit and died. Amy gave a shudder. The pit must be just ahead on the left.

At the place where they'd slid off the road there were no trees between the road and the pit. They could look straight down its sheer sides.

'Wow!' John peered into the foggy, dark space. 'It's enormous.' He jumped off Mustard, picked up a stone and hurled it out into the fog. After a long pause they heard a faint splash.

Amy slid off Classy's back and stared at the deep skid marks in the gravel. 'This is the place,' she said. 'The horse ran in front of our car. Mum jammed on the brakes and we skidded off the road.'

John was peering over the edge. 'The pit must be full of water,' he said. 'I wonder how deep it is?'

'Too deep. Don't go too close. The gravel is loose – you could slide.' Amy reached out a hand.

'I can't see much anyway. The fog . . . Amy, look at the fog!'

Amy turned round. While they had been staring into the pit, the fog had stalked up behind them. The trees on the other side of the road were just dim grey shapes. The road itself was a wall of white.

Amy felt as thought a cold white hand had gripped her neck. 'We'd better get back,' she said, swinging up on to Classy's back. John climbed on Mustard and they started back up the road. At first they could see each other, then Mustard surged ahead.

'He wants to run,' John called. 'See you back at the stable.'

The sound of his hoofbeats faded away and Amy was alone in the fog. Classy clopped along, shaking her head at the strange white stuff closing in around them.

Amy patted her neck. 'It's okay, Classy.' Her voice sounded loud and strange in their cocoon of fog. This might be one of her last rides on Classy, if Victoria had her way . . .

At that moment, Amy heard more hoof-beats. At first she thought it was John, riding back. Then she realised that the hoofbeats were coming from behind, fast and powerful.

She glanced over her shoulder, but she could see nothing. The hoofbeats were louder.

'Come on, Classy,' Amy urged the little mare with her heels.

Classy surged forward. They seemed to fly over the ground.

Still the horse behind was gaining on them. Now Amy could hear the snorting and blowing of a huge animal. She did not dare to look, just gripped Classy's sides with her legs and hung on.

Classy tore up the hill, seeming to sense the curves in the road. Somewhere, just ahead, was the old stone bridge.

The pounding hoofbeats were close behind as they rattled over the bridge and surged up the hill beyond. Gasping for breath, Amy bent low in the saddle to help Classy gain a little speed.

Now the other horse was so close she could hear the creak of its saddle – the horse had a rider! Amy's breath came in a ragged gasp. There was no way she could outrun whatever was pursuing her.

And then, suddenly, it was looming beside her. A tall figure swirled out of the fog. A voice thundered. 'Slow down!'

Amy sucked in a gulp of air that was almost a sob. She eased the pressure on Classy's sides. Her little mare slowed to a smooth, floating canter.

Amy turned to look at Nicholas, sitting tall in the saddle, on Prince.

'I thought maybe Classy was running away with you,' he panted. 'I've been trying to catch up with you since the quarry pit.'

You frightened the life out of me, Amy thought. Why hadn't Nicholas called out, to tell her who he was? Had he deliberately tried to terrify her? Perhaps cause an accident?

The sun was coming over the hills to the east and beginning to light the road. Amy was shaking with relief as she saw the shape of the barn ahead through the fog, and then the gates, and then the house and the riding ring.

The others were already doing their morning chores as they rode up to the barn. Victoria looked annoyed as Amy dropped off her horse, exhausted.

'Did you have a nice ride with Nicholas?' she said sarcastically.

'I didn't go for a ride with him!' Amy gasped.

'Don't try that stuff on me,' Victoria tilted her nose in the air. 'You're always trying to make Nicholas notice you. He was furious when he found out you and John had gone out for a ride without asking permission. So of course he went after you.'

'I couldn't care less if Nicholas noticed me,' Amy said wearily. Her legs were shaking after her hard ride.

'You look as white as a ghost,' Victoria peered at her. 'What happened out there? Did your spooky horseman give you a scare?'

'Leave her alone,' John muttered, as he passed with a bucket of grain. 'You have all the charm of a pit viper, Victoria.'

'Well, she's such a scared rabbit,' Victoria said. 'I'll bet she did think she saw a ghost

– in broad daylight!' She laughed nastily. 'Don't you remember what those girls at the horse show said? It's only on *moonless nights* you have to be afraid!'

'Amy's not afraid,' John said. 'I'll bet she could stand on that road on the darkest night and not bat an eyelid.'

'How much would you bet?'

'Whatever you want!'

John and Victoria stood, hands on hips, nose to nose. 'She'd never do it – go out there, by herself, on a dark night and stand by the road. Never!' Victoria said.

Amy didn't like the sound of this.

'Would you be willing to stop agitating to sell Classy if you lost this bet?' Caroline joined in. She winked at Amy over her shoulder.

Victoria glared at Caroline. 'What's Classy got to do with it?' she demanded.

'Oh, come on,' Caroline cried. 'We know you just want to get rid of Classy because you're jealous of what a great team she and Amy make.'

'Yes, come on,' John taunted. 'If you win the bet, Classy goes. If Amy wins, she stays.'

'What happens to Classy is not up to me . . .' Victoria said, her chin in the air.

'We all know it is,' Caroline said. 'One word from you to the Campbells and they'd drop the idea of selling her.'

Amy was listening dumbly, powerless to open her mouth.

'Hurry up, Nicholas is coming. Do you want to bet, or not?' John whispered.

'Yes, all right. I'll bet.' Victoria glared at Amy. 'She'll never have the nerve to go out there at night.'

'What about it, Amy?' John looked eagerly at her.

At that moment Sheila Campbell came into the barn with a man in a battered cowboy hat. 'This is Mr Bradley, the horse dealer,' she announced. 'He's come to take a look at Classy.' Sheila's face was unhappy and she didn't look at Amy.

The four campers watched as Mr Bradley opened Classy's stall and ran his hands over her and checked her teeth and feet. Amy had groomed her with special care after their hard ride and Classy looked her best.

'I think I have a buyer for you,' Bradley nodded. 'I can't get you much for a horse that kicks, but there's a fellow in North Chadwick who thinks he could use her.

How about day after tomorrow? Could I pick her up?'

'That will be fine,' Sheila Campbell said, nodding.

Caroline and John looked back and forth, from Amy to Victoria. Victoria raised her eyebrows in a question.

'I'll take the bet,' Amy whispered passionately.

'Are you sure?' Victoria whispered fiercely. 'No backing out?'

'I'm sure,' Amy said loudly.

Sheila Campbell turned to them. 'What's up?'

Victoria cleared her throat. 'Uh ... I've changed my mind,' she said. 'I'd like Nicholas to give me a few more lessons on Classy. She's a ... great horse, and I don't want to give up, like some *coward*!' she looked pointedly at Amy.

The bet was on.

Sheila Campbell looked worried and relieved at the same time. 'I guess we don't have a deal, Mr Bradley,' she said. 'Sorry to have brought you up here for nothing.'

Mr Bradley was gazing around the barn. 'Oh, I don't mind,' he said slowly. 'I haven't been up here for ages. You don't see many of these big old barns, these days. This place has quite a history, but I suppose you know all about it . . .'

Nicholas's face looked like a thundercloud. 'We know you're a busy man, so . . .' He was trying to steer the horse dealer toward the barn doors.

'Maybe you didn't hear all the stories about this place,' Mr Bradley turned and peered around the barn again.

'No, and we don't want to,' Sheila Campbell laughed nervously. 'It's just a lot of superstitious nonsense.'

'That may be,' Mr Bradley said. 'And of course, you don't want to scare the kids right out of their riding breeches.' He paused. 'But people have seen strange things up here.'

Nicholas was now herding him towards the barn doors. 'Don't worry.' Mr Bradley shook off his hand. 'I can find my way out. Let me know if you change your mind about selling the horse.'

When he had gone, Nicholas wheeled to face them. 'Hurry and finish here,' he barked. 'You still have to muck out three stalls, and we have something important to tell you at breakfast.'

He followed his mother and Mr Bradley out of the barn.

Amy stared after him. How could Victoria think that bossy, overgrown teenager was some kind of a prize? Nicholas was too vain, too full of himself, and . . . there was something else. If Nicholas had ridden past them on the ghost road, why hadn't she heard him? The horse that chased her had come from the opposite direction to Sunset Trails.

'Don't bother to thank me for saving your precious horse,' Victoria sniffed to Amy. 'You still have to win the bet. I can change my mind about Classy.' She walked away, exaggerating her limp.

Amy ran to Classy's stall and buried her face in her mane. 'I'll do whatever it takes to save you,' she murmured. Whatever was waiting on the ghost road, she had to go out there and face it.

Twelve

They waited for a moonless night. A silver of moon shone for three nights in a row after Victoria dared Amy to stand on the ghost road, and the skies were clear.

Every night Amy got more nervous.

At the nightly camp-fires, Victoria added conditions to her bet. 'You have to stand beside the road for one whole hour,' she stated. 'No running back here like a scared rabbit.'

Meanwhile they all worked hard at riding lessons. Nicholas's 'important announcement' had been a horse show in a week's time. This would be their last chance to compete before the end of camp.

But Amy's mind kept coming back to the bet. At last, on the fourth day, heavy clouds covered the sun and it began to rain. Camp-fire was cancelled.

'We'll meet in the barn at midnight,' John whispered at dinner.

In the bunkhouse, Caroline had everything organised. 'Raincoat, boots, a flashlight – so you can find your way – a couple of chocolate bars to munch on, and a whistle, just in case you're in real trouble.' She pointed to a pile of gear on the end of Amy's bunk.

'Thanks . . .' Amy tried to grin.

'We'd better get some sleep now,' Caroline said cheerfully. 'I've set my alarm clock for eleven forty-five.'

Caroline's brisk, cheerful manner was beginning to get on Amy's nerves. It wasn't Caroline who was going to be standing out there in the rain, in the pitch dark . . .

Amy didn't sleep. She lay awake, listening to the drumming of rain on the roof, to Caroline's steady snore. When the alarm sounded, hours later, it was almost a relief.

The rain was coming down hard as they made their way to the barn. It was so dark that without a flashlight they wouldn't have been able to find their way. Amy shuddered in her raincoat.

Amy and Caroline waited at the barn

door for Victoria and John's pinpoints of light coming down the path.

'All ready for a night of terror?' Victoria threw a sarcastic look at Amy as she squooshed past her through the puddle in front of the barn.

Amy said nothing.

John whipped a plastic case out from under his raincoat. 'I brought my portable video game so we can play while we wait for you, Amy,' he grinned.

'I don't think we'll be here long enough to play games!' Victoria sneered. 'Amy's going to be running back inside in less than ten minutes!'

'I'm glad you think so,' Caroline said. 'You're going to feel so stupid when she wins this bet.' She handed her watch to Amy. 'Take this so you know when the hour is up.'

Amy shoved the watch in her pocket and went over to where Classy was standing quietly in her warm stall. The little horse gave Amy a loving nudge.

'You do understand that I'm doing this for you,' Amy murmured. Classy bobbed her head so Amy could scratch between her ears. The rain and damp had brought out the smoky smell in the barn again. When Amy inhaled deeply, the sharp burnt smell sent a cold trickle of fear down her spine. Prince was stomping around in the next stall. Once again, she thought of the hoof beats pounding on the roof. It was time to go but she didn't want to move.

'Are you chickening out before you even start?' Victoria's nasty voice came over the top of the stall.

Amy closed Classy's stall and walked to the barn door.

'Where are you going to stand on the road?' John asked, as he opened the door for her.

'Just past the fork in the road, where it goes down towards the bridge,' Amy told him, trying to keep the tremor out of her voice. 'Victoria, will you do something for me?'

Victoria glared at her suspiciously. 'What?'

'Make sure Nicholas doesn't ride after me this time. Keep your eye on Prince, and make sure he stays in his stall.'

'Don't worry,' Victoria promised. 'There'll be no midnight rescue on Prince for you.'

'Good!' Amy said, and stepped out into the darkness.

The branches of a sheltering pine protected Amy from the worst of the driving rain. She dug Caroline's watch out of her pocket and shone her flashlight on its face. Forty minutes to go. She could hear nothing but the rain and the wind in the pine boughs. The space under the tree smelled of wet pine needles.

When the hoofbeats began as a distant drumming on the wet road, Amy felt a chill shoot down her spine, a knot of sickness in her stomach.

This time, it could not be Nicholas. The others were in the barn watching Prince.

Amy huddled in her raincoat as the sounds came nearer. Terror gripped her, making it impossible to move.

The others waited in the big, shadowy barn. Suddenly, the doors burst open, letting in a gust of wind and rain.

Amy stood in the open doorway of the barn. Water streamed down her face, part tears, part rain. Her hood was thrown back, her wet hair was plastered to her head.

'It is twelve forty-five,' Victoria crowed. 'You're fifteen minutes early. You LOSE!'

'Amy, what happened?' Caroline cried. She caught Amy as she staggered through the door.

'What did you see out there?' John asked, rushing over to her.

Amy's eyes were wild and staring. She was shaking from head to foot and gasping for breath.

'She's faking,' Victoria announced. 'Can't you see it's just an act?'

'Ooo-h I'd like to get *you* out there on that road in the dark . . .' Caroline said fiercely.

'Any time,' Victoria flounced towards the barn door. 'I'm not afraid of some spooky old ghost on a horse.'

'Prove it!' Caroline challenged. She was still holding Amy upright.

'Just name your day . . . or night. In the meantime, she loses.' Victoria pointed at Amy. 'I knew she wouldn't last an hour. Well, this has been a bore, and I'm going to bed.' She flipped up the hood of her raincoat and disappeared, leaving the barn doors flapping open.

John ran to close them. Amy's teeth were still chattering. Her knees buckled under her.

'Okay, kiddo, tell us what happened.'

Caroline helped Amy down on a pile of loose hay.

'It was . . . aw-awful,' she stammered.

'Tell us everything,' Caroline tucked a thick horse blanket round Amy's shaking body. John came and sat beside them, peering anxiously into Amy's face.

'I heard him coming,' Amy's eyes were wide with terror. 'The whole ground shook as he rode toward me. I smelled smoke through the rain. I had my flashlight on, so I could see your watch, and I just froze – I couldn't turn it off.'

'What did you see?'

Amy swallowed hard. 'I . . . tried to turn the light off, but while I was trying to find the switch, I shone it on the road, and . . .' She stopped and licked her dry lips.

'It's okay, go on,' Caroline urged.

'It was on a big black horse,' Amy gulped again. 'And it had this huge sword in its hand and it was slashing the sword back and forth in front of it as it came . . .'

'Did you see its face?' Caroline gasped.

'That was the worst. It had on this hooded thing, like a c-cape,' Amy stammered. 'And when the light shone on it, it turned towards me, and . . . it had *no face*. No eyes, no nose, and no mouth. There was just a blank space where the face should have been, and then . . .'

Amy gulped and shivered again. 'Then I got the light off, but it was too late. The black horse was almost on top of me, and . . . it was dark, but there was something glowing, under the rider's arm. I was so scared I thought I would be sick.'

'Go on,' John cried.

'He was still swinging the sword with the other arm, and the glowing thing . . . I think it was his head!' Amy had her head on Caroline's shoulder. She took a deep breath and lifted her face. 'I tried to run, but my feet wouldn't move. I could feel the wind from the sword slashing back and forth. I fell down.'

'Then what?' John gasped.

'Then . . . the horse reared up, and whinnied – it was such a horrible sound, and then . . . it just wheeled away, and I heard it go thundering down the road.'

'Wow!' John's eyes were huge. 'A horseman with no face . . . with his head under his arm!'

At that moment Classy whickered in the darkness.

Amy suddenly sat up straight. 'What's Victoria going to do about Classy?' she gasped. 'I lost the bet.'

'I guess you didn't understand,' Caroline told her. 'The bet is still on. Only this time it's Victoria who bets she can face the ghost on the road.'

Amy shuddered. 'I wouldn't send my worst enemy out on that road.'

'Oh, yes, you would,' Caroline said firmly. 'I don't know what you saw, but something really scared you. Now we're going to send old snoot-face Victoria out there and make sure she has the fright of her life!'

'What do you mean?' Amy was listening now.

'I mean, between the three of us, we can make sure Victoria sees the headless horseman . . .'

John looked excited. 'That is a great idea!'

'You don't know what you're messing around with,' Amy said. She got up and walked over to Classy's stall. 'I'm sorry I let you down,' she whispered. She turned to her friends. 'I couldn't – I just couldn't go out there again.'

'There will be three of us,' Caroline

reminded her. 'Together, we'll make a great ghost.'

'And I know where we can get a sword,' John said.

'Poor Amy,' Jo sighed, as Charlie paused and reached for another can of drink. 'She must have hated the idea of going out on that road again – even to get revenge on Victoria.'

'It's funny that she's the only one who ever sees or hears the ghostly rider,' Alex said. She stirred the fire with a long stick and a stream of sparks shot up into the dark sky.

'Well, maybe she *is* psychic,' Louise suggested. 'You know, the kind of person who sees supernatural things. That's what those girls at the horse show said, that only certain people could see the ghost.'

'Maybe the ghost was trying to send a message through Amy,' Jo agreed. 'Sometimes ghosts come back because they have unfinished business . . .'

'Like cutting off people's heads with a sword?' shuddered Louise. 'Maybe you're right. Hurry and finish your drink, Charlie. We want to know what happens next.'

'Nobody else wants a drink?' Charlie asked, peering into the cooler. There's orange in here, and cola, and grape . . .'

'CHARLIE!!' three voices chorused.

'Just keeping up the suspense,' she grinned, snapping the cooler shut. 'Okay, where were we?'

Thirteen

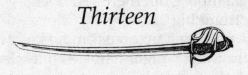

'John had this great idea about a sword,' Jo prompted. 'Oh, I love stories like this, where people plot revenge!'

'But first they had to get the sword,' Charlie reminded them. She settled back down in her comfortable spot on the sand. 'Okay, here goes.'

'Wait a minute!' Alex suddenly untangled her long legs from the sleeping bag and stood up. The others watched her walk away from the fire towards the lake.

'Alex? What are you doing,' Jo cried. 'We finally got Charlie back into the story . . .'

'Are you going swimming?' Charlie asked.

'Shhh!' Alex's whisper came back from the darkness. 'I thought I heard something in the water again.'

They all stopped talking. The buzz of crickets was loud in the still night. Then there was a soft *plop*, *plop*, like footsteps, wading along the shore.

'Something's out there!' Alex said quietly. 'Something big . . .'

'Is it sneaking up on us?' Louise shivered. All her worst nightmares about sleeping outside in the dark were coming true.

'Listen, there's two of them,' Alex hissed. They were quiet. The soft splashing continued, coming along the edge of the water.

'Alex! Get back here!' Charlie said. 'It might be the skunks!'

'Too big. And I don't think skunks like water.'

'Maybe two-legged skunks,' Jo whispered. 'Like Stephen and his friends from down the lake.'

'Get out of here!' Charlie bellowed, at the top of her voice.

The splashing footsteps stopped. There was a moment of heart-stopping silence. Then two pairs of evil, glowing eyes turned towards them, reflecting the firelight.

These were not human eyes.

In the next second there was a huge splashing and bobbing of gold flashing eyes. The sleepover gang threw themselves backwards, out of the way of four pairs of flying hooves. The animals thudded away in the trees. They were just two white blurs in the dark as they disappeared.

'Oh, glory, what was that?' Alex breathed, lifting her head.

Charlie was on her feet laughing and dancing around on the sand. 'Deer! Didn't you see their white tails scudding away. It was just a couple of deer coming down to the lake to drink. Oh, wow! I really thought it might be ghost horses there for a minute.'

'It just proves that what you see in the dark can look like almost anything,' Jo sighed. 'Maybe that's what happened to Amy. Anyway, Charlie, *please* get back to the story.'

With sighs and squirms the Sleepover gang settled themselves again. It was getting cooler on the beach and Jo and Louise climbed into their warm down bags.

Charlie found her comfortable spot on her own sleeping bag, hugged her knees and leaned close to the fire to keep warm. Her voice got low and thrilling as she returned to the story of the Sunset Trails Riding Camp.

Amy dreamed she was riding a powerful

black stallion. With just the slightest pressure from her legs it would rise into the sky and fly over the tops of the hills and trees.

She opened her eyes as the dream faded. The air smelled fresh after the rain and Amy lay there, remembering the exhilarating feeling of riding the great horse in her dream.

Suddenly she heard a tapping at the bunkhouse shutter.

John's anxious face was peeking in the window. 'Hey, Amy, Caroline, wake up.'

'John?' Amy sat up in astonishment. 'What time is it?' If John was up, it must be very late. He was always the last at the barn for chores.

'It's almost six. Can I come in?'

'NO!' Caroline roared from her bed. 'What are you doing here?'

'We have a lot of planning to do. We have to be ready for the next dark night, to fool Victoria. I want to show you the list I made.'

Caroline looked at Amy. She shrugged. 'He might as well come in. Give us a minute to get dressed,' Amy called, and John's head disappeared.

John's list, when he bustled into their

118

bunkhouse and showed it to them, was impressive.

1. Get a cape.
2. Make a head.
3. Get a strong flashlight.
4. Get the old sword off the fireplace.
5. Find out if we can ride in the dark!

'I thought it would be better if Victoria could ride down the road, and then Caroline could chase her on Joker, dressed up as the headless horseman.' John explained.

'Brilliant planning, but what if the *real* headless horseman comes along,' Amy shuddered. 'I know you don't believe me, but I *saw* something on that road.'

'You don't have to come,' Caroline said. 'John and I can do it. John could hide, down by the pit, and then pop out as Victoria comes tearing by. And then I could ride up, and show her she's been running from a fake ghost. I can't wait to see her face at that moment,' Caroline grinned.

'No,' Amy shook her head. 'If you and John are really going to do this – I want to be there.'

Of all the items on John's list, the head was the most trouble. To make it they needed flour, water, strips of newspaper, and a large balloon. Working by flashlight in their bunkhouse, Amy and Caroline made thick, gooey paste with the flour and water. Then they moulded it into a head, using a balloon. The final touch was straw, stuck on for hair.

'It looks so real!' John said when they showed him the finished head. 'Now, shine the flashlight inside.'

The hollow eyes shone from within. 'That's exactly right,' Amy said shakily. Caroline put on the cape they had stitched together from grey blankets, and held the lighted head under her arm. In the shadowy bunkhouse, she looked frighteningly like the hooded figure Amy had met on the road.

John and Caroline were having fun, Amy thought, because they didn't believe in the ghostly rider. She dreaded another night on the road. 'How are you going to get the sword from the fireplace?' she asked.

'We'll leave the sword to the last, in case Nicholas or Sheila miss it,' John explained. 'We'll wait until we're sure it's going to be a dark night to snatch it. Then we can put it back the next day.'

Finally, after three days of clear skies, the sky clouded and it looked as though another storm would sweep over the hills.

'Hey, Victoria,' Caroline called that morning as they warmed up their horses. 'Remember our dare?'

'Of course,' Victoria called back. She was putting Marvel through his paces. The big, easy-going pony showed the good effects of being groomed and cared for by Victoria every day. He had a light in his eye and looked less bored in the dressage ring. Victoria rode up beside Caroline and glared at her. 'Are you still sticking up for that sissy, Amy?'

Caroline kept her eyes straight ahead. 'Tonight should be good and dark. How about riding down the old abandoned road as far as the quarry pit at midnight?' she asked.

'Sure,' Victoria tossed her head. 'Riding sounds good.'

'And if you can't, if you run away, then you'll stop complaining about Classy?' Caroline insisted.

'If she behaves herself . . .' Victoria said with a nod, riding ahead.

'Then it's agreed. Meet at the barn tonight, like we did before!'

*　　*　　*

'Now for the sword,' John said. 'All we have to do is wait until Nicholas and his mother are both out of the house.'

'There might be a chance while Victoria is having her lesson with Nicholas and Sheila is busy in the barn,' Caroline suggested.

Amy was quiet. The whole thing felt wrong. Victoria was still limping and threatening to call her mother and complain about Classy. Who was to say she would keep her end of the bargain if they succeeded in making her look and feel like an idiot?

At four o'clock they collected John from his bunkhouse and stole in through the back door of the house.

The living-room was full of shadows. Over the big stone fireplace the ancient sword flashed silver.

'Do you think they'll miss it?' Amy said nervously, staring at the long blade.

'In all this clutter?' Caroline looked around the busy room. 'I don't think so.'

'Watch out the window for anyone coming,' Amy said. 'We don't want to get caught!'

John stood on the hearth stone, a large slab of marble, and tugged at the sword.

'It's fastened on tight,' he grunted. 'I can't move it.'

Amy peered at one end of the sword. 'There seems to be some kind of metal clip holding it.' She wiggled the sword hilt. 'We need a knife to prise it out.'

Caroline ran to the kitchen for a sturdy carving-knife.

Amy inserted the knife carefully between the sword and the stone of the fireplace and pulled back on the handle. The clip flew out with a grating noise. Something fell on the hearth at her feet – a folded square of paper.

'Here,' Amy handed the knife to John. 'Prise out the clip at your end.' She supported the hilt of the sword as he worked, and reached down to pick up the yellowed newspaper that had been wedged behind it.

'Quick! Nicholas is coming.' Caroline had been watching at the side window.

'I've almost got it,' John panted, prising the clip with all his might. 'Help me, Amy.'

'There's no time,' Caroline moaned. 'He's coming up the walk.'

Amy leaned on the knife, John gave a final wrench and the sword popped free. He ducked into the corner between the fireplace and the wall, with the sword held behind him.

Amy shoved the paper in her pocket. It was too late to try to leave. Nicholas was ducking through the low front doorway.

He looked surprised to see them. 'What are you two doing here?' he asked. He seemed incredibly tall in this low-ceilinged old farmhouse.

'Just looking for food,' Amy said. She knew they must look guilty. Better to have some excuse rather than say nothing.

'We've got the afternoon munchies.' Caroline nodded in agreement. 'Can you help us find something to eat?' If they could get Nicholas in the kitchen it might give John time to scuttle out of the back door with the sword.

'Why this sudden hunger?' Nicholas said. 'You two hardly eat anything.'

'I guess our appetites just caught up with us,' Amy shrugged. 'At home, I eat like a horse.'

'Speaking of horses, I'll get some more carrots for the horses while we're here,' Caroline said, rummaging through the metal bin where carrots were stored, making as much noise as possible.

'How are Victoria's lessons going?' Amy asked quickly. Through the kitchen window she could see John scurrying away from the house, holding the sword in front of him.

'Fine,' Nicholas said. He seemed puzzled by her sudden interest in Victoria's progress. 'But she's still afraid of Classy, and the horse knows it. She won't perform for Victoria like she does for you.' He paused. 'I'm sorry, but it looks as if we still might lose Classy . . .'

John had disappeared. Amy gave a quick sigh. 'Well, thanks for trying, anyway. We'd better be going.'

'Didn't you want something to eat?' Nicholas frowned.

'No, we'd better wait for dinner,' Amy said. 'Come on, Caroline. I want to brush Classy down.' She shot a glance at Nicholas as they raced from the kitchen. He looked confused.

After dark, John appeared at the bunkhouse with the sword. 'It's got some initials on it.' he pointed to the silver hilt. 'It must be a real antique.' He swished it back and forth in front of him. 'What did the paper say?'

'We haven't read it yet,' Amy told him. 'The paper is so crumbly it almost fell apart in my pocket. It must have been up there for years!'

She carefully smoothed out the folds of the newspaper.

'*The Bolton Valley Banner*,' Amy ran her finger along the top line of type. 'It's a local paper.'

'Look at the date,' Caroline pointed. 'September 6, 1948. It's almost fifty years old. That's how long the sword must have been over the fireplace!'

'Wow! Check the headline!' John's eyes glinted behind his glasses. 'HEADLESS HORSEMAN RIDES AGAIN.'

The four of them poured over the yellowed page, riveted by the large black headline and the story under it:

West Chadwick: Does the ghost of Andrew Acton ride these hills? Andrew Acton was a young farmer at West Chadwick in 1778, during the War of Independence from Britain. His neighbours knew he was loyal to the King. Returning home to his wife and infant son one night, Andrew Acton saw his barn on fire. A troop of revolutionary soldiers were burning the farms of the loyalists.

But what the soldiers didn't know was that Acton's young wife was hiding in the barn with six-month-old Joshua Acton. Andrew Acton discovered their charred remains in the burnt-out barn and the baby's blanket caught on a tree branch near the house. He rode off in the night with the blanket, swearing revenge for his loved ones.

But the soldiers were waiting on the road. In the hand-to-hand battle that followed, Andrew Acton was beheaded with one swipe of a sword belonging to a revolutionary named Gareth Simmons. That sword was left at the farmhouse, which has been torn down and rebuilt several times since that night one hundred and seventy years ago. People who have tried to live at the old Acton farm have reported strange things in the area . . .'

'Don't read any more,' Amy urged. 'I know what they've seen. I've seen it too.'

There was silence as John and Caroline stared at her.

'He wants revenge for the death of his wife and baby,' Amy said in a hushed whisper.

'That's why he carries the sword,' John fingered the blade of the sword in his hand. 'Hey, look at these initials – G.S. – Gareth Simmons!'

'That part of the story must be true,' Caroline's round eyes were wide. 'Gareth Simmons killed Andrew Acton with this sword more than two hundred years ago!'

'And Andrew's ghost can't rest until he gets even,' Amy finished. 'Sunset Trails must be the old Acton farm. I can prove it to you tonight, if you still want to go through with this.'

'I guess *now* they'll listen to Amy,' Louise said. 'They know she wasn't just imagining the ghost on horseback!'

'He was a real person,' Alex said in a hushed voice. 'Andrew Acton. Imagine how he must have felt that night . . .'

'Whoever he was, I wouldn't want to meet him,' Jo shuddered. 'Did they carry on with their plan to scare Victoria, after that?'

Fourteen

Charlie reached for another chocolate bar, peeled back the paper, snapped off a chunk for herself and handed the rest around.

'That was the problem,' she said. 'They had to decide whether to go on with their plan, or not.' She crumpled the chocolate wrapper and tossed it in the fire.

'Keep going with the story,' Jo urged. 'Tell us what happened next.'

'And don't stop to eat,' Louise added.

Charlie leaned forward to put some more sticks on the fire. As it blazed up, they could all imagine the burning barn on that night of terror. Charlie's storytelling voice held them all motionless as she went on.

'I vote we call it off,' Caroline shook her head. 'This is too weird. I never believed in ghosts – and I don't particularly want to start tonight.'

'But what about our bet with Victoria?' John pointed to the sword, cape and head on Amy's bunk. 'We've got everything ready. I vote to carry on.'

Caroline was silent for a moment. 'I don't know. What do you think, Amy? You have the final vote here. You've seen . . . what might be out there.'

'I think it's too late to call it off, now,' Amy said slowly. She felt as though they were all puppets, with a 220-year-old ghost pulling their strings. She was the channel – the one who had heard the horse on the roof, and seen the ghostly rider. There was something the rider had to do. And they had to play their part – no matter how dangerous or terrifying it was.

Amy glanced at the fake head with its hollow eyes and shivered. 'We might as well lug all this stuff down to the barn and hide it, while we have the chance.'

That night, none of them slept. At midnight, Caroline met Victoria at the barn, as arranged.

'Where are the other two?' Victoria demanded.

'Amy's trying to wake up John,' Caroline told her. She pulled the clipping out of her pocket. 'Victoria, I think you should look at this.'

Victoria glanced at the headline: HEADLESS HORSEMAN RIDES AGAIN. 'Where did you get this?'

'We found it in the house.' It wasn't a lie, or the complete truth.

Victoria gave it another scornful glance. 'Well, I think it's stupid. Everybody knows there are no such things as ghosts. This must be a joke, or they're talking about an old movie . . .'

'It's from 1948!' Caroline said. 'Look at the date.'

Victoria shrugged. 'Who cares?'

'Okay,' Caroline threw up her hands. 'We just wanted to warn you.'

'To scare me, you mean,' Victoria scoffed. 'I'm not impressed. Well, I'm ready to go. Aren't Amy and John going to see me off?'

'They'll be here when you get back – in one hour, not less.'

Victoria lifted her tack from the hook in the tack room, and led Marvel out to the crossties. Quickly she slipped on his bridle, threw the saddle blanket and saddle over his back and tightened the girth.

'All right,' she said, hoisting herself up on Marvel's back. Do you have a watch?'

'Mine says twelve-twenty,' Caroline said. 'I'll see you in an hour.' She heard Marvel's hoofbeats clop off down the road.

Alone in the big barn, Caroline knew she had to hurry. If Victoria got down the road too far ahead of her, the whole plan would fall apart. She quickly saddled Joker, her fingers fumbling with the buckles.

Hurriedly, she slipped into her long dark cape, tucked the head and sword under her arm and swung up on the saddle. It was going to be very hard to manage all this stuff and ride at the same time, she suddenly realised. And somehow, she still had to get the flashlight inside the head for the illusion of the ghost rider to be complete.

Amy and John raced down the tree-lined road, their flashlights bobbing. 'This is far enough,' panted Amy. 'We'll wait here.'

Round the next bend was the quarry pit.

Amy thought she could almost feel the cold from its depths.

They crouched in the trees at the side of the road, and flicked out their lights.

'Listen,' John said. 'She's coming.' They could hear hoofbeats pounding down the road towards them.

'Get ready, John. She's coming fast!' Amy cried. In another moment Victoria would come sweeping round the bend.

Instead, they heard a sudden shout, then a crashing and snapping of branches somewhere to their left.

'She's ridden into the woods,' Amy gasped. 'Marvel is so spooked he's left the road.' She grabbed John's arm. 'They're headed straight for the quarry pit.'

'Victoria!' she screamed. 'Stop! You're too close to the pit.'

'STOP!' John added his cry to hers as they both turned and ran in the direction of the fleeing horse. Their flashlight beams lit the dense undergrowth, the trunks of huge maples, the tangled evergreen branches in their path. The dark forest ended suddenly and their flashlights lit empty space.

'Victoria!' Amy screamed again. The empty pit echoed her voice.

Amy stopped, her breath coming in jagged gasps.

'H . . . here!' came a quavering cry.

Amy and John swung their lights to the right.

It was Victoria, clinging to Marvel's neck like a small, frightened child. She was only a few steps from the crumbling edge of the pit.

'I'm afraid to m-move,' she stammered.

Amy leaped from Classy's back and ran forward to grab Marvel's reins. 'Gently, big boy, step back.' She kept her voice level. 'Good boy, step back.'

Victoria still clung round his neck. Her proud face was streaked with tears, and she was clutching a fragment of cloth in her hand. 'Something . . . spooked Marvel. I couldn't hold him. He just charged into the woods. I heard you call, but he wouldn't stop and then . . .' She wiped her eyes with the rag in her hand.

'Someone on a huge black horse cut in front of me. It made Marvel slow down, b-but . . .' Victoria was really crying now. 'But whoever it was just couldn't stop and rode right over the edge.'

Amy and John stared at each other, horrified. *Caroline*!

Fifteen

Amy fell to her knees and crept to the lip of the quarry pit. Now she could definitely feel the chill from the dark water far below. She shone her flashlight into the blackness.

'Caroline!' Amy shouted with all her might.

There was no answer.

'We've got to get help,' Amy scrambled to her feet. 'Come on Victoria, we need your horse.' They started to run back through the tangled brush.

'Do you think that was *Caroline*?' Victoria said in a shocked voice. 'But her horse isn't that big. And what was she doing out here on a horse?'

'We'll explain later . . . come on!' They plunged back towards the road, Victoria leading Marvel by the reins.

When she reached the road, John grabbed Amy's arm. 'Look,' he gasped. 'There's some-one coming.'

They snapped off their lights. At that moment, the clouds parted overhead and for a moment a full moon shone down on them. A dark horse was picking its way carefully along the road. They saw the cold gleam of a sword blade.

Amy felt a scream rising in her throat. At any second that sword would start to flash and cut.

'Hey – who's there?' came a voice.

'Caroline!' Amy gulped in relief. She switched on her light. 'Oh, Caroline, it's you.'

'Did you find Victoria?' Caroline asked anxiously. 'I'm afraid I really spooked poor Marvel. He bolted after one look at me.'

'She's here,' Amy said. They all gathered on the road in the moonlight.

'I don't understand . . .' Victoria looked from one to the other.

'It was a trick,' Caroline said, holding out the fake head. 'I was supposed to scare you and send you galloping down the road. And I guess I did.' She paused. 'But after you ran off, someone else galloped past me on a big black horse. Did you see it?'

Victoria's voice was cracked with fear. 'Whoever it was saved my life. But they're down there . . . in that pit! It might be Nicholas!'

Amy shivered. 'I don't think it's Nicholas, but we should go back to Sunset Trails and make sure. I'll ride behind Caroline, and John, you go on Marvel behind Victoria.' She was already swinging up on Joker's back.

At the barn, they threw themselves off the horses and raced inside. A loud whinny greeted them, and a long black nose peered over the stall.

'Prince!' Amy cried. Quickly she checked up and down the rows of stalls. 'Prince and Classy are here, and Mustard, and Piper, Sheila's horse. They're all here.'

'Then who saved Victoria?' John looked baffled. 'And who rode over the edge of the pit?'

'The horse that followed you into the woods,' Amy insisted, 'tell me about it.'

Victoria gaped at her. 'It towered over me,' she said. 'I could feel its size and . . . power, but I couldn't see much – just a hooded shape on its back. But I heard the harness jingling, and the bit in its mouth, and I felt . . .' she looked at them, embarrassed. 'I suddenly felt so sad.'

Amy remembered the tears on Victoria's cheeks.

'And there's one more thing,' Victoria stammered. 'Th-there was a smell – on the horse, and all around me. Like smoke.'

Victoria put the rag she had been clutching in her hand up to her nose. Then she stared at it, as though she had forgotten it was still in her hand. 'It smelled like this . . .' she thrust the scrap of cloth at Amy.

'It's some kind of old knitted material,' Amy said slowly. 'It looks like a piece of blanket.'

The scrap of cloth, when they spread it out, was knitted wool. It could have been blue at one time. Now it was marked with dark stains.

'The baby's blanket from the burning barn!' Caroline gasped.

Amy felt a chill down her spine.

'After more than two hundred years?' John looked at it. 'I don't think so.'

Amy's eyes were fixed on Victoria's face. 'Strange things have been happening around here,' she shook her head. 'Where did you get this?'

'It was hanging on a bush, after . . . after the horse stopped me from going over the edge.'

Amy put the scrap of knitted wool to her nose. A familiar scent made her head reel. 'It smells like old burnt stuff,' she said.

'That's right,' Victoria nodded. 'That's what I smelled in the woods.'

'I don't think we need to wake up anybody to go for help,' Amy said breathlessly. 'I don't think anything alive went over the edge of the quarry pit.'

That night, for the first time since coming to the camp, Amy slept soundly. She had no dreams. She woke up without the smell of smoke in her head, feeling lighter, as though a weight of sadness had lifted from her shoulders.

The image of the ghostly rider turning Victoria's horse away from the pit, and then soaring into darkness himself, filled her mind. Maybe the ghost of Andrew Acton had fulfilled his task – and not by getting revenge for his dead wife and baby. Maybe by saving Victoria, he had found peace.

The sun shone brightly on the old barn when she joined the others for morning chores. Nicholas was riding Prince round the outdoor ring, taking him over the jumps. Amy walked into the barn. Once more it seemed like a peaceful place of sunbeams and contented horses.

Victoria was showing the others her sore leg. One pant leg was pulled to her knee. Amy went over to look.

'But how did you make it look so bruised?' Caroline said. 'It was positively purple. It's still purple.'

'Indigo dye, from a new jean vest,' Victoria said. 'It washes off. Look . . .' She dipped a sponge in a pail of water and wiped her shin. The purple faded and disappeared.

'What did I miss?' Amy asked.

'Hi!' Victoria glanced up at her. 'I was just showing them how I faked Classy's kick.'

'You faked the kick?' Amy gasped.

'The way *you* faked the headless horseman,' Victoria grinned. 'You guys aren't the only masters of disguise around here . . .' She pointed to the ghostly paper head in the corner.

'Are you going to tell Sheila?' Amy asked.

'If I have to . . .' Victoria shrugged. 'But maybe she won't sell Classy if I just stop complaining about her.'

'What made you change your mind?' Amy asked, astonished.

'I realised how stupid I was to be jealous of you, that's all,' Victoria said. 'After Nicholas rescued me last night, I know he cares.'

Amy looked quickly at John and Caroline. 'Nicholas saved you?' she repeated.

'Sure. Oh, I got caught up in your ghost story games last night,' Victoria tossed her head. 'It was dark, and I was scared. But I really don't believe in ghosts and anyway, I have proof it was Nicholas who rode over the edge.'

'Proof?' Amy couldn't believe her ears.

'The poor guy has a terrible cold this morning,' Victoria said triumphantly. 'That's what you get from leaping into cold water in the middle of the night!'

'She figures Prince swam ashore,' John shrugged.

Amy was speechless. She walked back out to the riding ring and watched Nicholas fly over a jump on Prince. *What a horse*! she thought for the hundredth time.

John and Caroline came up beside her to watch. 'I suppose Prince could have survived such a leap,' Amy murmured. 'But why did he look so warm and dry when we got back to the barn?'

'Not like a horse that had been running hard and diving off cliffs,' Caroline agreed. 'But maybe Nicholas wiped him down.'

'It's possible,' John agreed. 'Maybe there is no ghost, after all.'

At that moment, Sheila Campbell called them to breakfast. John and Caroline ran towards the house, but Amy saw Nicholas waving to her, and waited until he rode up to the fence. Nicholas's face was pale and his eyes were watery. 'I wanted to talk to you . . . ACHOO!' he sneezed violently.

Amy looked up at him. 'Okay.'

'This next competition is really important to the camp. If we do well the word will get out and we should get more campers next year.'

'We'll try,' Amy promised.

'Good. There's something else. You and I haven't got along very well,' Nicholas said. 'It's this ghost story business.'

Amy felt a guilty pang. 'I won't talk about it any more,' she promised.

'No!' Nicholas sneezed again. 'That's what I wanted to say. I've changed my mind. You see we bought Sunset Trails for almost nothing. People were frightened away by the ghost that is supposed to haunt this farm. Local people warned us we would never succeed here, and then when you said you saw a horse on the road, and heard a horse at night, we thought it was beginning all over again.'

'I understand,' Amy said, 'but I don't think the ghost rider will be back.'

'It's – ACHOO! – okay!' Nicholas reached in his pocket for a handkerchief. 'I think the stories might be good for us. Kids like ghosts. A good ghost story might make the camp seem more exciting, as long as it wasn't too scary . . .'

Amy stared hard at Nicholas. 'Do you really mean it?'

Nicholas nodded.

'But you don't believe in the ghost, do you?' she asked.

'Of course not!' Nicholas smiled his old, charming smile. 'There's no headless horseman, right, boy?' He leaned forward and patted Prince's neck, and the tall black horse whinnied as if he agreed.

'Kids might like the story,' Amy said slowly. She wondered how much Nicholas knew about their midnight ride. 'But I'm not sure about the ending . . .'

And I probably never will be, she thought,

as she watched Nicholas ride away and canter Prince towards the next jump. He gathered his legs under him and flew over the rails as though he had wings. She might never know the whole truth. But somehow, she was now part of the story, too.

'And that,' said Charlie, staring into the flames, 'is why Amy goes back to Sunset Trails every year. She's still reliving what happened on the ghost road that night.'

'Whew!' Alex whistled. 'Did the headless horseman ever come back?'

'It hasn't so far,' Charlie said. 'Amy showed us the little scrap of bloodstained blanket. *That* was spooky. She leaves it on a bush beside the barn every time she goes back, in case the ghost comes for it. And the sword is back over the fireplace again.'

'What happened to Nicholas?' Jo asked.

'Oh, he's still a Grand Prix rider,' Charlie said. He was away competing in Europe last summer when I went to camp.'

'And Victoria?'

'She gave up riding for skiing,' Charlie laughed. 'She discovered that skiing instructors are cute, too. Caroline works at a stable all summer, but the most surprising person

144

is John. He ended up moving out west and becoming a junior rodeo rider!'

Jo got up to pace the beach in front of the fire. 'I know how Amy feels about these hills up here,' she said. 'When I come to your cottage I get that same restless feeling. Like my life has been too ordinary—' She stopped pacing and stared into the darkness.

'Like I said,' Charlie nodded. 'It's easy to believe in the unbelievable. These hills are old, old worn down mountains, with a lot of secrets hidden in them.'

'Look,' Jo said. 'There's another camp-fire on the beach.'

They all got up to take a look. Just down the lakeshore another fire was burning with a fitful, twinkling light.

'Is that at Stephen's place?' Jo asked suddenly.

'Probably,' Charlie said in disgust. 'Copy-cats!'

'I've got an idea,' Jo cried. 'Let's sneak up on them, in the canoe.'

'You mean, crash *their* sleepover?' Alex asked.

Sixteen

'Why not?' Jo danced around the fire. 'We could just glide along in the canoe, really close to the shore, hear what they're saying, and then surprise them.'

'Jo, you never give up, do you?'

'I just want to see his face . . .'

Alex laughed. 'It might be fun. Come on, Charlie. Let's do it. I can't sleep after that story anyway. I'm going to hear thundering ghost horses all night.'

'Are you *seriously* thinking of paddling across the lake, in the dark?' Louise's voice was hoarse with disbelief. 'I *couldn't*. Every time I dipped my paddle in the water I'd be thinking about those lake monsters down there.'

'That gives me an idea!' Jo gripped Charlie's arm. 'Does Stephen know the lake monster legend?'

'Of course, we both grew up hearing those stories.'

'Then why don't *we* pretend to be the lake monster, creeping up on *them* . . .' Jo's eyes were gleaming in the firelight. 'We could scare the life out of them. What would we need . . . ?' She glanced around their campsite.

'We could put a groundsheet over us, and crouch down in the canoe,' Alex suggested. 'Then we'd look like one long snake.'

'Brilliant – but we need a head!' Jo cried.

'With eyes on stalks,' Charlie reminded them.

'Okay. Two flashlights, stuck in the ends of one of those long foam tubes we use for swimming.'

'Perfect!' Jo cried. 'They'll even wobble around a bit. It will be so realistic.' She was hugging herself with glee. 'I can't wait to see Stephen's face. He's going to be so scared.'

Louise was still hunched down by the fire. 'I think you're all crazy,' she muttered. 'It's dangerous to canoe in the dark.'

'I promise we'll keep close to the shore,' Charlie said. 'There's no danger.'

'Come on, Louise,' Alex added. 'You've been so scared of the lake monster. Now you'll get to *be* a lake monster, Besides, it's no fun if we aren't all in it.'

A few minutes later they shoved Charlie's red canoe, loaded with all their gear, into the calm lake. Jo sat in the front to paddle, with the flashlights and eye stalks shoved into the narrow prow in front of her. Alex sat behind, and Louise, still protesting, took the centre. Charlie shoved off, climbing into the stern to steer.

The canoe wobbled dangerously.

'Careful,' Alex hissed. 'No sudden movements. We're pretty low in the water.' She put her hand over the side. In the dark she could only feel a few centimetres of freeboard between the lake and the top edge of the canoe.

Louise was paddling in a state of frozen terror. Each time she dipped her paddle into the dark water of the lake she expected it to be grabbed in the jaws of the lake monster. There was something so eerie about the way the canoe slipped along with no sound except the soft splashing of the paddles.

'I can't see the shore,' she whispered to Jo. 'Where are we?'

'We're getting close,' Jo whispered at last. She had been watching the camp-fire light growing steadily closer. 'Try to slice the water with the paddle so you don't splash.

We don't want them to hear us coming until the last second!'

'Get ready with the eyes,' Alex whispered back. 'Here's the ground sheet. Try and pull it over you.'

The canoe rocked and wobbled as they tried to adjust themselves to new positions.

'Crouch down, we're almost there,' Jo said. 'I'm going to switch on the lights. Ready?'

On the shore, four boys were crouched round their camp-fire, getting ready for a feast. At the sudden vision of a huge monster speeding towards them over the water, its eyes waving wildly on twin stalks, they leaped up in terror.

'Eeeeaugh!' The tallest, Stephen Piggott, stumbled backwards with an open can of beans clutched to his chest. The others scrambled to get away, howling with fear. In his panic, Stephen tripped over a log and fell under a cascade of beans.

There was a burst of laughter from the monster. 'Oh . . . oh, look at them!' Jo, who had the best view from the front of the canoe, was having a helpless fit of giggles.

'Jo!' Alex screamed. 'Stop rocking the boat! We're going to . . . ARGGGH!'

There was a frightened scream, a tremendous *splash*! and the canoe was upside down in the water.

Louise came up, kicking and spluttering under the floating groundsheet.

'It's all right,' she heard Alex shout. 'It's shallow. You can stand up.'

'Speak for yourself,' Charlie cried. 'We're not all as tall as you!'

Finally, four sopping wet bodies dragged the half-filled canoe up on the shore near Stephen's camp-fire. Jo was still laughing.

'You looked so funny,' she choked. 'Just before we tipped – your face! With beans all over it!'

Stephen stared down at her. 'You scared the wits out of us, sneaking up like that! It's not very nice to laugh at people.'

'Now you know how it feels,' Jo said.

Stephen Piggott looked confused. Then he blushed. 'The thing is . . .' he wrinkled up his nose and a bean dripped off his eyebrow. 'I wasn't such a great rider, either, when I was learning. In fact, I fell off quite a lot, didn't I, Charlie?'

'All the time,' Charlie nodded. 'You were hopeless.'

'So the thing is,' Stephen repeated. 'I had

no business laughing at you this afternoon and I'm sorry.'

'That's okay,' Jo giggled. 'Sometimes, you just can't help it.'

'We're soaked,' Alex said. 'We'd better empty the canoe and get going.'

'Would you like to come and get dry at our fire,' one of the other boys asked. 'We've got beans, and sausages.'

'Oh, no!' Alex grabbed Charlie's arm. 'We should get back,' she said quickly. 'Your mum doesn't know where we are.'

'But if you're having a fire another night,' Charlie said wistfully, we could come back . . . if there's any beans and sausages left. We've got lots of biscuits and marshmallows.'

'Sure. We'll be here all week.'

'So will we,' Jo was helping Louise dump the water out of the canoe. She stopped and looked up at Stephen. 'Are you going riding tomorrow?'

Stephen shrugged. 'Maybe.'

'Well, if you do, we'll see you there.'

They launched the canoe and waded into the water to climb aboard. There was no use worrying about wet clothes now.

'I hate to say "I told you so",' Louise said, as they paddled away, 'but that's twice you've fallen into the lake in one night!'

'It doesn't matter,' Jo sighed happily. 'I was face to face with Stephen when those flashlights went on. Seeing the look on his face was worth anything!'

Another Hodder Children's book

THE WEIRD EYES FILE
A Hunter & Moon Mystery

Allan Frewin Jones

Meet next door neighbours, Beth Hunter and Hal Moon. Beth's imagination's always getting her into trouble and Hal's practical jokes always backfire . . . but when mystery stares them in the face, Hunter and Moon are on the case!

Beth disturbs a burglar outside her room. What was he after? She's got nothing of value. There's no sign of a break-in and nothing's been taken. The police don't believe her – was her imagination playing tricks? Only one *weird* pair of eyes saw what really happened . . .

THE ALIEN FIRE FILE
A Hunter & Moon Mystery

Allan Frewin Jones

Meet next door neighbours, Beth Hunter and Hal Moon. Beth's imagination's always getting her into trouble and Hal's practical jokes always backfire . . . but when mystery stares them in the face, Hunter and Moon are on the case!

Beth spots strange lights from her window late at night. Glowing green in the distance, then disappearing. She's convinced there's been an alien landing. But Hal saw them too and he's not so sure. Until a midnight encounter leaves them both thinking . . .

ORDER FORM

HUNTER AND MOON MYSTERIES
Allan Frewin Jones

0 340 67818 6	THE WEIRD EYES FILE	£3.50	❑
0 340 67819 4	THE ALIEN FIRE FILE	£3.50	❑
0 340 67820 8	THE SKULL STONE FILE	£3.50	❑
0 340 70962 6	THE TIME TRAVELLER FILE	£3.50	❑
0 340 70963 4	THE THUNDERBOLT FILE	£3.50	❑
0 340 70964 2	THE STARSHIP FILE	£3.50	❑

All Hodder Children's books are available at your local bookshop or newsagent, or can be ordered direct from the publisher. Just tick the titles you want and fill in the form below. Prices and availability subject to change without notice.

Hodder Children's Books, Cash Sales Department, Bookpoint, 39 Milton Park, Abingdon, OXON, OX14 4TD, UK. If you have a credit card you may order by telephone – (01235) 831700.

Please enclose a cheque or postal order made payable to Bookpoint Ltd to the value of the cover price and allow the following for postage and packing:
UK & BFPO – £1.00 for the first book, 50p for the second book, and 30p for each additional book ordered up to a maximum charge of £3.00.
OVERSEAS & EIRE – £2.00 for the first book, £1.00 for the second book, and 50p for each additional book.

Name...

Address...

....

....

If you would prefer to pay by credit card, please complete:
Please debit my Visa/Access/Diner's Card/American Express (delete as applicable) card no:

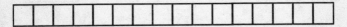

Signature...

Expiry Date...

ORDER FORM

THE SLEEPOVER SERIES
Sharon Siamon

0 340 67276 5	THE SECRET ROOM SLEEPOVER	£3.50	❑
0 340 67277 3	THE SNOWED-IN SLEEPOVER	£3.50	❑
0 340 67278 1	THE HAUNTED HOTEL SLEEPOVER	£3.50	❑
0 340 67279 X	THE CAMP-FIRE SLEEPOVER	£3.50	❑

All Hodder Children's books are available at your local bookshop or newsagent, or can be ordered direct from the publisher. Just tick the titles you want and fill in the form below. Prices and availability subject to change without notice.

Hodder Children's Books, Cash Sales Department, Bookpoint, 39 Milton Park, Abingdon, OXON, OX14 4TD, UK. If you have a credit card you may order by telephone – (01235) 831700.

Please enclose a cheque or postal order made payable to Bookpoint Ltd to the value of the cover price and allow the following for postage and packing:
UK & BFPO – £1.00 for the first book, 50p for the second book, and 30p for each additional book ordered up to a maximum charge of £3.00.
OVERSEAS & EIRE – £2.00 for the first book, £1.00 for the second book, and 50p for each additional book.

Name...

Address..

....

....

If you would prefer to pay by credit card, please complete:
Please debit my Visa/Access/Diner's Card/American Express (delete as applicable) card no:

Signature..

Expiry Date..